DOVER
GOES
TO
POTT

Chief Inspector Dover novels
Dover One
Dover Two
Dover Three
Dover and the Unkindest Cut of All
Dover Goes to Pott
Dover and the Claret Tappers

DOVER GOES TO POTT

Joyce Porter

A Foul Play Press Book

The Countryman Press, Inc.
Woodstock, Vermont

Copyright © 1968 by Joyce Porter

This edition first published in 1990 by Foul Play Press,
an imprint of The Countryman Press, Inc.,
Woodstock, Vermont 05091.

ISBN 0-88150-173-5

Printed in the United States of America
10 9 8 7 6 5 4 3 2 1

To
Margaret Daragon Wishart
with much gratitude

Chapter One

A HUNDRED years or so ago Pott Winckle, now a small undistinguished town, was a small undistinguished village. This metamorphosis was brought about by the happy juxtaposition of a modest deposit of china clay and a man called Daniel Wibbley. Daniel Wibbley exploited the china clay with such energetic genius that he put Pott Winckle on the map, provided it was a large-scale one. Today all but a handful of the town's population depends, directly or indirectly, for its livelihood on the Wibbley Ware Company Limited, a name to be conjured with in the world of domestic sanitary equipment.

To Daniel Wibbley the First must be given the credit for the original vision. Having discovered his patch of china clay he examined the glories of Wedgwood, Spode and Doulton, and sensibly lowered his sights. Being a practical man he made up his mind to specialize in chamber pots and with half a dozen underpaid workers began manufacturing. Since he produced a reasonably priced, reliable article which satisfied a basic human need, his business flourished modestly. It was left to his son, Daniel Wibbley the Second, to break into the big time. Daniel Wibbley the Second stopped bothering his head about the quality of his chamber pots and devoted all his energies to improving the quality of his advertising. His full-page spreads in all the popular newspapers were at once the wonder and the despair of his Edwardian contemporaries. His most successful series, Famous Buildings, caused a minor scandal with its smudgily drawn pictures of Balmoral, Buckingham Palace, Windsor Castle and Holyrood cowering under the banner caption 'There's one under every bed!' Still, whatever it did to loyal sensibilities, it sold chamber pots and Daniel Wibbley was soon enlarging his father's factory and branching out into wash basins, baths and water closets. His son, Daniel Wibbley the Third, continued the expansion. His products, propelled by ruthless salesmanship, highly dubious business methods and saturation advertising, penetrated the four corners of the world. By his middle forties Daniel Wibbley the Third was a millionaire tycoon and he held the town of Pott Winckle in the palm of his large smooth hand.

The autocracy was an indirect one. It was so powerful that it didn't need to be anything else. Daniel Wibbley didn't have to stand as a councillor to control the town hall. Daniel Wibbley hadn't set foot in a church for donkey's years but ministers of every denomination in Pott Winckle felt they had him as an invisible witness at their sermons. Even Labour parliamentary candidates were chosen with one eye on Daniel Wibbley, an undisguised Conservative. After all, the entire Socialist selection committee worked in his factory.

Mr Wibbley wasn't exactly popular with the citizens of Pott Winckle but they certainly knew he was there. Either he paid their wages or he paid the wages of their customers. If his works closed down, the town would die. Pott Winckle knew this, and so did Daniel Wibbley.

With this sort of background it wasn't surprising that a fair old panic broke out amongst Pott Winckle's policemen when it was discovered that Daniel Wibbley's only child, a daughter, had been murdered. The superintendent promptly had one of his queer turns and everyone knew there was no hope of recovery until all the fuss had died down and any cans that were to be carried had been picked up by somebody else. The station sergeant, who had received the original telephone message, was shaking like an aspen leaf and the chief inspector, left right up the breech by his superior's defection, turned pale. Fifteen years before, as a raw young constable, he had stopped Daniel Wibbley's chauffeur for speeding. The case had never come to court, of course, but the chief inspector still had nightmares about it. Was history going to repeat itself in an even more horrible form?

'Shove it upstairs!' advised the station sergeant breathlessly.

'Get rid of it! If you don't have nothing to do with it they can't blame you, whatever happens, can they?'

The chief inspector glared at him irritably. You could see why this nit had never got beyond three stripes on his fat arm. 'How can I shove it upstairs, you fool? The super'll have lashed himself into a coma by now. If you think he's going to stage a miracle recovery just to pull this one out of the fire for … '

The station sergeant shook his head. How this sloppy burk ever got himself promoted he'd never know! 'Not the super, the Chief Constable!' He reached for the telephone. 'Here, I'll get County Headquarters for you.'

'What difference is that going to make? The Chief Constable'll only shove it back in my lap. You know what he's like. It's Pott Winckle's crime and Pott Winckle must deal with it. It's what he calls giving the man on the spot a sense of responsibility, the stupid basket!'

'Scotland Yard!' wheezed the station sergeant, unexpectedly burgeoning with ideas. 'Ask him to fetch the Yard in! Then you don't need to do nothing, 'cept stick a copper on guard until the Yard men get here. They'd appreciate that, the Yard men would. They're always griping about us local chaps mucking their crimes about before they can get their hand on them themselves. Go on—it's the perfect let-out!'

The chief inspector grasped anxiously at the tempting straw. 'Do you think the Chief Constable'll play?'

''Course he will! He won't want to tangle with Big Dan any more than we do. But put it to him diplomatic like. There's no need to mention that his son's just started at Wibbley's in the accounts.' He winked.

'You're a cunning old devil,' said the chief inspector gratefully. 'If this works we might save our bacon yet!'

The station sergeant picked up the telephone and asked to be put through to the Chief Constable. 'Just so's you remember who it was what first thought of it,' he said complacently as he handed the receiver over.

9

That was at about half past six on a damp, early autumn evening. At thirteen and a quarter minutes past two on the following morning a train rattled to a halt in Pott Winckle's deserted railway station. Two men climbed stiffly down on to the platform. The bulkier one, the one who wasn't encumbered with suitcases, turned up the collar of his overcoat and grimly surveyed his surroundings from beneath the brim of a shabby bowler hat. This was Chief Inspector Wilfred Dover of New Scotland Yard, not that New Scotland Yard was likely to boast about it.

Dover pursed his tiny rosebud mouth and screwed up his beady little eyes. ' 'Strewth!' he said.

His assistant, Detective Sergeant MacGregor, struggled with the suitcases and sighed.

'Why', demanded Dover peevishly, 'is there nobody here to meet us?'

'I don't know, sir, I'm afraid.'

'In that case, laddie, get your skates on and find out!'

'Yes, sir.' With resignation MacGregor put the suitcases down on the platform and hurried off into the wavering shadows. Dover watched him for a moment and then shuffled over to the nearest bench and sat down.

A whistle blew, the engine coughed, a door slammed and the train pulled wearily out of the station.

Dover huddled deeper into his overcoat and closed his eyes. He'd barely had time to doze off before his sergeant was back again. Reluctantly he raised his heavy lids.

'Oh,' he said, 'well, at least you've been able to find a porter.'

There was an embarrassed pause. Even in a bad light there is little excuse for confusing a uniformed chief inspector of police in all his glory with one of the less glamorous employees of British Rail.

'Er – no, sir,' – MacGregor, as so often in the past, rushed in to the rescue – 'this is Chief Inspector Bream, sir. He's temporarily in charge of the Pott Winckle police, I understand. He was waiting for us in the waiting room. He hadn't realized that the train had come in.'

A disparaging sniff came from the bench.

'Your train was over two hours late,' explained Chief Inspector Bream, wanting to kick himself for making excuses but unable to stop, 'and it was getting really nippy out here on the platform and, as I was telling your sergeant here, I just thought I'd ... ' His voice tailed off. Dover had closed his eyes again.

Chief Inspector Bream looked questioningly at MacGregor. MacGregor just failed to shrug his shoulders and, in a strictly non-committal voice, completed the introductions. 'And this, sir, is Chief Inspector Dover.'

'Oh,' – Chief Inspector Bream floundered unhappily – 'well, er – welcome both of you to – er – Pott Winckle. I – er – hope your visit will be a very – er – successful one.'

Dover rose abruptly and unexpectedly to his feet. 'I'm just about whacked,' he announced. 'I'm off to bed. Come on, MacGregor, get moving. Even if he isn't a porter he can give you a hand with the bags.'

It was one of Chief Inspector Bream's more humiliating experiences. None of the firmness and command which he was to display so eloquently in his later reconstructions of the scene came to his aid now. In the moment of truth all he could do, to his eternal shame, was pick up the heavier of the two suit-cases and scurry, protesting feebly, after the humped and menacing figure of Dover.

He caught up with him at the station exit.

'Is that', demanded Dover, jerking his head at a gleaming Rolls-Royce parked directly opposite, 'a taxi?'

'Good heavens, no!' Chief Inspector Bream's voice soared to a squeak. 'Look, you really must hang on for a minute and let me explain.'

'Well,' said Dover, pausing as if to the manner born while a uniformed chauffeur came round to open the door for him, 'if this is a police car, all I can say is that I've been sweating my guts out all these years in the wrong bloody force! Drive straight to my hotel, my man!'

In the end, however, right prevailed and Chief Inspector Dover was not driven straight to his hotel, chiefly because the chauffeur had already been given his orders and he was accustomed to doing exactly what he was told.

'All right,' said Dover testily as the Rolls purred along through the dark streets, 'the car belongs to Daniel Wibbley. So what?'

'Mr Wibbley is the father of the girl,' explained Chief Inspector Bream, grateful even for a morsel of Dover's attention.

'What girl?' asked Dover, jabbing his stubby fingers at a mini-console of buttons which he had found on the arm rest.

'The girl who's been murdered!' wailed Chief Inspector Bream as the window on his side of the car rolled silently up and down.

'Oh, *her*!' sniffed Dover. 'Hey, look – it's a cocktail cabinet!'

'Mr Wibbley is a very influential man in Pott Winckle, very influential. And the Chief Constable was most insistent that I should impress upon you that this case must be settled with expedition and discretion.'

'My favourite brand, too!' said Dover, holding a glass full of whisky appreciatively up to the light. 'I wonder if he's got any fags going spare? My, this is the life, isn't it, eh?'

'The Chief Constable says he doesn't want any slip-ups. He said that several times. And he wants you to co-operate fully with Mr Wibbley, even if it is a bit unorthodox. Mr Wibbley is a very important man and he'll want to be kept fully in the picture.'

'Oh,' said Dover in a tone of mock disappointment, 'he's only got cigars! Well, beggars can't be choosers, eh? Got a light, MacGregor?'

'I really don't think', Chief Inspector Bream said faintly, 'that you ought to ... Well, the chauffeur might be watching and ... '

Dover cheerfully told his brother officer what he could do with the chauffeur and stuffed half a dozen enormous cigars in his pocket for, as he jocularly put it, a rainy day.

Surreptitiously Chief Inspector Bream wiped his brow.

'Well, old fish,' said Dover, settling back comfortably in the cushions, 'hey—do you get that, MacGregor? Bream—fish! Get it?'

'Yes, sir,' muttered MacGregor, 'I get it.'

'Well, don't look so blasted boot-faced about it, then! That's the trouble with you, you've no bloody sense of humour. Some people are never satisfied. A Rolls-Royce, free cigars, whisky—what more do you want? Oh, I'm going to enjoy this case, I am!'

'If you would just listen to me!' whined Chief Inspector Bream, now getting as close to tears as a chief inspector ever does.

'This woman who got herself croaked,' said Dover, 'was she married?'

'Yes, she was.'

'Husband knocking about?'

'Well, yes. Actually he was the one who found the body.'

'So what are you sweating about?' asked Dover, leaning across and spilling the ash from his cigar all over MacGregor's knees. 'He's the nigger in the woodpile. You just want to clap the handcuffs on him and shove him inside. He'll be your man all right.'

Chief Inspector Bream shuddered at the mere thought of arresting, in cold blood, the great Daniel Wibbley's son-in-law on a charge of murder. 'I don't think it's quite as simple as all that,' he ventured.

' 'Course it is!' scoffed Dover. 'The world's full of husbands bumping off their wives. It's what you might call one of the laws of nature.'

'Oh, come now!' Chief Inspector Bream accompanied this gentle chiding with a most unfortunate laugh. 'That's a bit sweeping, isn't it?'

Dover twisted round in the close confines of the back seat of the Rolls and scowled ferociously at Chief Inspector Bream. 'Are you trying to teach me to suck eggs, mate? That's ripe, that is! Do you hear that, MacGregor? Here's a blooming glorified traffic warden who's spent his life looking for lost poodles and telling people what time it is trying to teach me my job. That's good, that is! Me, that was already C.I.D. when this yokel was trying to find out which end of his whistle to suck!'

Chief Inspector Bream went scarlet up to the ears and Sergeant MacGregor gazed miserably out of the window. Neither of which happenings staunched the flow of Dover's eloquence. He proceeded to open up every festering old sore which had ever existed between the detective and uniformed branches, and then rubbed salt in them. The bewilderment of one of his fellow passengers and the mortification of the other made no difference to Dover. He hadn't wanted to come to Pott Winckle in the first place and as for wasting his time on this mucky little murder case—well, you could stuff that! Naturally somebody had to pay for Dover's ill temper and, since Chief Inspector Bream was handy, he would do as well, if not better, than anybody else.

It was thanks to this prolonged outburst of petulance that Dover eventually found himself face to face with Daniel Wibbley knowing, if possible, slightly less about the murder of the tycoon's daughter than he had in London.

The bereaved father was an impressive figure as he stood in his spacious study surveying his visitors. He was a big man but in good physical trim and with a carefully tended look about him. His hair was greying appropriately at the temples and the blue of his eyes was exactly matched by the dominant colour in his silk Paisley smoking jacket. The room in which he stood echoed the theme of unobtrusive good taste, backed by money. After all, when one's family fortunes are based on chamber pots and one's name is Daniel, one cannot be too careful in eschewing any hint of vulgarity.

'So you're the detective from London, are you?' he rasped, eyeing Dover up and down with ill-disguised surprise. Most people, it must be confessed, evinced a certain amount of simple disbelief when they saw Chief Inspector Dover for the first time. He chimed so ill with the popular romantic image of a senior policeman. He was too fat, too shabby and too surly-looking. Added to which he had a paunch, chronic dyspepsia and acute dandruff. Where were the keen grey eyes, the high intelligent forehead, the wide generous mouth crinkling slightly at the corners in a benevolent smile? Not, it was only too obvious, in Wilfred Dover's lowering, heavy-jowled mug.

'Hm,' said Daniel Wibbley.

Dover glared bleakly back at him and hoped he was going to be invited to sit down soon. All this standing around did his poor old feet no good at all.

'Well,' said Daniel Wibbley, 'I don't think we need to have a committee meeting about this. Bream, you and the sergeant can wait outside. If you want any refreshment I dare say you'll find some beer and sandwiches in the kitchen.' He watched them leave the room. 'I hope', he observed, turning to Dover, 'that that man of yours can be trusted to keep his hands off the maids. It's difficult enough as it is to get servants these days, don't you find?'

Dover, sycophant and snob that he was, smarmily agreed.

'Whisky?' asked Daniel Wibbley. 'And there are some sandwiches for you by the fire. Roast beef, I think. Perhaps you would like to take your overcoat and hat off before we sit down.'

Dover took the hint and draped his overcoat over a chair, being careful not to crush the cigars which he had already purloined from his gracious host.

For the next hour or so Daniel Wibbley spoke and Dover ate. This made them both happy.

'I want to get one or two things straight right at the beginning,' Daniel Wibbley announced from the depths of his deep leather armchair. 'On a man-to-man basis, you understand. You probably appreciate the position I hold in Pott Winckle. My father and grandfather made this town and I keep it going. This naturally gives me a certain amount of power. Within broad limits I can do what I want in Pott Winckle and with Pott Winckle. Unfortunately Pott Winckle is at times not the whole world and outside the confines of the town while I may have influence I do not have total control.'

'Quite, quite,' said Dover, through a roast-beef sandwich.

'A murder trial', Daniel Wibbley continued, 'will be held in the Assize town. I cannot hope to get the consideration from a Queen's Bench judge and his jury that I would from the local magistrates. That being the case I shall have to deal with this tragic business as any ordinary man would. Not even I'—he smiled bleakly—'can hope to manipulate the entire majesty of the Law.'

Dover blinked. His jaws moved slowly up and down. He'd got a right one here all right!

'Nor', said Daniel Wibbley vehemently, 'must there be the slightest suspicion that I have even contemplated assisting the course of Justice. That would ruin everything! This is why I insisted, when the Chief Constable called round to see me, that Scotland Yard should be called in without delay. The local police are no doubt perfectly capable of tracking down my daughter's murderer, but in so doing we might be providing the defence with a loop-hole. There would always be some malicious and ill-informed people who would hint that my wishes had played an undue part in the course of their investigations. With you in charge of the case, Dover, there can be no such suspicions. When you present your findings the whole world will be forced to admit that they are entirely unbiased and based on solid fact. You follow my line of reasoning?'

'Oh yes,' said Dover and casually waved his empty glass.

'The decanter is by your elbow. Kindly help yourself. Now, I propose to put you in the picture as far as my daughter's death is concerned. No doubt Bream has already given you some information so you must forgive me if I repeat what you already know.'

'Don't both about me,' said Dover graciously. 'Just you pretend that I don't know a blind thing.'

'That's very kind of you. Please feel quite free to ask any questions if you wish clarification of some point.'

'Thank you,' said Dover without the faintest trace of irony.

'Not at all. Well now, where shall I start? My daughter was called Cynthia and she was twenty-one years of age. She resided at Sligachan, 17 Birdsfoot-Trefoil Close—part of a housing estate built for owner-occupiers of the lower-middle classes. She had resided there since her marriage. The house' —Mr Wibbley repressed a shudder—'is being purchased on a mortgage. My daughter, at the age of eighteen, married a young man called Perking, John Perking. He was twenty-one years old at the time and the son of one of our store-room clerks.' Mr Wibbley suddenly stopped looking down his nose and glanced at Dover. 'Oughtn't you to be writing these details down in your notebook?' he asked sharply.

Dover's eyes shot open. 'Eh?' He always claimed that he concentrated better with his eyes closed and, in any case, it was really getting very warm there by the fire and he'd been up all night and ... 'Oh, a notebook?' The old master brain clicked over at top speed. 'No, no!' He smiled reassuringly. 'I don't bother with notebooks.' He tapped the side of his head with quiet confidence. 'I keep it all up here!'

'Really? Well, it is perhaps advisable not to have too much down in writing at this stage. Now, my daughter's husband is employed as the manager of a small branch of a travel agency which opened here in Pott Winckle several years ago—when the working classes began to frequent the Costa Brava for Wakes Week. The Safari-Agogo Travel Agency, situated at 42 Mary-Anne Wibbley Street—our main shopping centre.

'My daughter, unlike most of the childless young wives of the social stratum into which she had married, did not go out to work. Not, I may observe in passing, out of any consideration for my position in the town but principally because at Benbowly Abbey College, where she was educated, they do not make a point of training their pupils for employment as shop assistants or milk roundswomen. Yesterday afternoon, therefore, she was, not surprisingly, at home. There she was murdered. In the front room, as I believe it is called. She was beaten to death with, probably, a poker which formed part of a set of fire-irons, also located in this same front room. The police surgeon—the only person incidentally who has been permitted to enter the house since the discovery of the murder —confirmed that my daughter was indeed dead, gave his preliminary opinion as to the cause of death – the poker, and estimated that the death had occurred between four thirty and six thirty that afternoon. You will no doubt be somewhat surprised that he could not be more precise.'

The pause lasted just a fraction too long.

'Eh?' gulped Dover, opening his eyes very wide and trying to look intelligent. 'Oh yes, I am. Very surprised.'

'This imprecision was the result of the proximity of a large fire in the front-room hearth. The body had fallen very close to the fire and this made a precise calculation of the time of death somewhat difficult as, so I am given to understand, the temperature of the corpse is a valuable clue and, amongst other things, affects the onset of rigor mortis. However, unsatisfactory as it is, that will be the medical evidence: death took place between four thirty and six thirty.

'The discovery of my daughter's lifeless body was made by her husband on his return from work. According to a brief statement he made to the police – on my advice he has not been questioned further and is now staying with his married sister at 25 Canal Bank Street under unobtrusive police surveillance – according to his statement he examined his wife to see if she was still alive and if he could render any aid and then he essayed to summon assistance. His own telephone, which stands in the hall, had apparently been torn out from the wall by the wires. He was thus obliged to leave the house and avail himself of the services of a public telephone kiosk, situated at the corner of Birdsfoot-Trefoil Close and Navelwort Drive. By some minor miracle this instrument had just been restored after the latest act of senseless vandalism and my daughter's husband was thus enabled to contact the Central Police Station at six twenty-nine p.m. A police car was dispatched immediately to the scene of the crime, to which my daughter's husband had also returned.'

'I see,' said Dover, and struggled to sit up a bit straighter in his chair. 'Well, that's given me something to be going on with. I ... '

'I haven't finished yet,' said Mr Wibbley coldly.

'Oh,' said Dover.

'I should like at this point to give you my opinions on capital punishment. I consider capital punishment a good thing. We are told in the Bible—an eye for an eye and a tooth for a tooth and to let the punishment fit the crime. I am not myself a deeply religious man but on this point I wholeheartedly concur with the Church's teaching. Unfortunately, as no doubt you are aware, capital punishment has been abolished in this country—a most retrograde step, in my opinion.'

'You're dead right there!' agreed Dover with a sudden burst of enthusiasm. 'Disgusting, I call it! Well, it ties your hands, doesn't it? You can't scare the life out of some rotten little yobbo by waving life imprisonment at him, can you? And where's the incentive for us coppers, that's what I want to know? In the old days you didn't mind taking a bit more trouble over a job if you knew the villain was going to get his neck stretched at the end of it. It gave you something to work for, if you see what I mean, and topping ... '

'Quite,' said Mr Wibbley, eyeing Dover with some distaste. 'I am glad we see eye to eye on this question, more or less.'

'I reckon they ought to bring the birch back, too,' muttered Dover resentfully. 'And the cat. Give 'em a taste of their own medicine, that's what I say. It's these kids, you know. They're the trouble. They're not brought up to have any respect for law and order these days. Why, you'd hardly credit it, but there's some of these vicious young devils that'd thump a copper as soon as they would their own mothers—and chiv him, too, if they get half a chance. And why not? What happens to 'em if, by some miracle, we do nab 'em? They come up in front of some silly old beak who says it's all because they weren't potted properly when they were kids and it's not ... '

Even Dover, no more sensitive than the average pachyderm, felt a definite drop in the temperature. There were some things you could mention in the presence of Mr Wibbley and some it was advisable to avoid. Potting, even when used in the strict horticultural sense, fell in the latter category. Most of Pott

Winckle shared Daniel Wibbley's touchiness. Lavatory jokes were out and, even at the height of two world wars, the enemy were always referred to as Germans.

Mr Wibbley registered his disapproval of Dover's faux pas by a slight tightening of the jaw and then resumed his monologue as though the Chief Inspector had never spoken – a touch of consideration for the feelings of others which shows that gentlemen can be made as well as born.

'As a businessman,' said Mr Wibbley, 'I pride myself on being a realist. And we must be realistic on the question of capital punishment. In the present situation there is no hope at all that the murderer of my daughter will expiate his crime on the gallows. We may deplore this state of affairs but we cannot alter it. I therefore consider it no more than my simple duty as a father to ensure that this man is made to suffer the maximum punishment that the law allows.'

'Life imprisonment,' said Dover helpfully.

'As you say, life imprisonment. And what, precisely, does that mean?'

'Damn all, if you ask me,' grumbled Dover. 'Ten years inside on the average, so they say. And most of that in one of these open prisons if you play your cards right. Bloody mollycoddling! Mind you, there's a few they keep locked up for a heck of a sight longer but, on the other hand, there's some they let loose on society after as little as a couple of years, say. It makes you sick! Walking about without a care in the world in two years when you ought to be swinging with your heels six inches off the ground!'

'And who is responsible for these anomalies?'

'Eh?'

'Who is responsible for keeping one murderer in prison for thirty years and for letting another one out after only two?'

'Ah, well, that's the Home Secretary, of course. Mind you, he gets a lot of advice from all these snivelling do-gooders like psychiatrists and prison chaplains and what have you, and if they say let 'em out he lets 'em out.'

'I doubt if the matter is quite as simple as that,' said Mr

Wibbley rather patronizingly. 'As a Justice of the Peace as well as an active supporter of the movement to restore the death penalty, I have made it my business to study the question in some depth. However, basically, you have the right idea. Periodically the case of every prisoner serving a life sentence is passed under review. All aspects of the matter are, so we are assured, carefully considered: the nature and motivation of the crime, the man's attitude towards it, his behaviour in prison and so forth. I am given to understand that criminals who have committed particularly brutal, vicious and callous crimes for gain and so forth are less likely to secure an early release than those who have murdered in a fit of ungovernable passion, for example. Now, I hope you are following my line of reasoning?'

'Oh, yes,' said Dover.

'Good! Then I can be confident of your full co-operation. We must ensure, Dover, not only that the murderer of my daughter is brought to public trial but that he is exposed as a cold-blooded, deliberate killer who should never again be allowed to contaminate decent society by his presence. There must be no half-measures, no sympathy for the accused, no understanding of his point of view, no suspicion that he is not as black as he is painted. He must not only be tried, he must be pilloried.' He must go down in history along with all the other murderous thugs whose very names make honest citizens shudder. This man must not only be sentenced to life imprisonment, he must actually serve it – until his dying day.'

Mr Wibbley paused dramatically and there was a squeaking of leather as Dover wriggled uneasily in his chair. The Chief Inspector was not one to become involved in his work, emotionally or otherwise, and he found Mr Wibbley's passionate oratory a bit embarrassing. He tried to lower the temperature.

'Well, that's fine, Mr Wibbley, but we've got one or two little jobs to get out of the way before we start talking about trials and verdicts. After all,' – he produced an unfortunate giggle – 'we've got to catch our murderer first, haven't we?'

Mr Wibbley waved an impatient hand. 'What on earth are

you blethering about? The identity of the killer is no problem.'

'It isn't?'

'I thought I had clarified the situation for you more than adequately!' snapped Mr Wibbley. 'Apparently your wits are not as nimble as one would have expected in a so-called expert. Your job is to ensure that the murderer of my daughter does not escape his just and, I trust, lengthy reward. Good heavens, man, everybody knows *who* he is! He's John Perking, my daughter's husband and my son-in-law.'

Chapter Two

'THAT marriage was doomed from its inception,' said Mr Wibbley with a loquacity which appeared, to Dover's increasing dismay, totally unaffected by grief, the lateness of the hour or any reasonable consideration for the feelings of others. 'I told my daughter so when the matter was first mooted but, these days, you can't tell an eighteen-year-old chit of a girl anything. She had the impertinence to accuse me of snobbery when I tried to point out to her that Perking was nothing more than a vulgar little upstart with his eyes firmly glued on the main chance. Anyone, except my daughter, could see that he was after her money – or, rather, after my money. However, I managed, I flatter myself, to thwart the young whelp there. When I realized that I could do nothing to stop my daughter – she even threatened to apply to the courts if I refused my consent – I sent for Perking and told him just precisely what the situation would be if he persisted: not one penny piece from me!

'My daughter was, of course, my sole heir and in time she would, naturally, have inherited my not inconsiderable business interests. But, until my decease, the responsibility for providing for her would, in the circumstances, fall entirely upon the shoulders of the man she married. I made it quite clear that they could expect no help from me. Perking was considerably shaken by this intelligence but he possesses a certain amount of crude cunning. He informed me in a very eloquent speech, which had obviously been pre-prepared, that he loved Cynthia, that he would be honoured to support her on the measly pittance he received from this travel agency, that he was sorry to have caused so much trouble between myself and my daughter, that wealth meant nothing to either

23

of them and that in time he trusted that my attitude towards him would become less suspicious and less antagonistic. You can see what his game was, of course?'

'Oh, yes,' said Dover, beginning to feel some sympathy for young Mr Perking. 'I expect he thought you'd come round in time and then he'd be in clover.'

'He didn't know me very well,' observed Mr Wibbley grimly. 'I am not a man who changes his mind easily. They were married in a registry office. I did not attend the ceremony. However,' he smiled unpleasantly, 'I did send them a wedding present: a complete bathroom suite. Our popular model. The de luxe one would have been a trifle pretentious for Birdsfoot-Trefoil Close.'

Dover propped his eyes open and tried to turn the monologue into a discussion. He wasn't much of a one for just sitting there and listening. 'But, if your daughter had no money, what did her husband murder her for?' In some matters Dover had a very one-track mind.

'That is what you are here to find out.'

'You didn't relent then and cough up a bit of the ready?'

'I did not! My daughter had made her bed with her eyes open. As far as I was concerned, she could lie in it. However, I must confess, there was one circumstance in which I might have been induced to change my attitude: if the marriage had produced a child. Naturally I could not have permitted a grandson of mine to be reared on a housing estate. A reconciliation would then have taken place. I am sure that my daughter and her husband both realized this and, I admit, I myself was counting on it. My daughter had to be taught a lesson but it was none-the-less embarrassing to have her living in comparative poverty in my town and practically on my doorstep. It would have gone very much against the grain to have accepted Perking as a member of my family but, for the sake of an heir, I would have made the sacrifice. I am not, thank God, a small-minded man.'

'But there was no pattering of tiny feet, eh?'

'None.'

24

'Perhaps they weren't trying?'

'Oh, they were trying all right! As far as my daughter was concerned, the glamour of attempting to exist on fifteen pounds a week must have been getting very thin. She knew well enough that there was no hope of getting any more unless she presented me with a son. Her husband knew it, too. But, after three years, there wasn't a sign. No one, I must admit, was more surprised than I was. Perking's attraction for my daughter was a purely sexual one. The girl was completely infatuated with him. On the rare occasions I have encountered the pair of them together, both before and after the marriage, they have behaved to each other with an amorousness which I found frankly disgusting. In my opinion, the young whelp is impotent. I made the same observation to my daughter some months ago and suggested that she might care to investigate the possibilities of having the marriage annulled. She refused, of course. However, I am a patient man. The seed had been sown. I have no doubt that before long she would have been giving serious consideration to the step I had proposed.'

'It's not', grumbled Dover, 'giving him much in the way of a motive, is it? By killing your daughter this Perking fellow's kissed a sweet goodbye to all hopes of fame and fortune, hasn't he? So, why did he murder her?'

'She may have threatened to get the marriage annulled.'

'Got any reason for thinking she did?'

Mr Wibbley shook his head. 'No, none. But I haven't seen her for several weeks. Her attitude might have changed considerably in that time.'

Dover sighed. All the sandwiches had been consumed and even the whisky was getting a bit low in the decanter. He would dearly have loved to bring this remarkable session to an end, but that prerogative looked as though it belonged to Daniel Wibbley.

'Is there a Mrs Wibbley?' he asked miserably. Not that he cared but it showed that he was taking an interest.

'We separated a couple of years after my daughter was born. My wife is a member of one of our chief local families – the

25

Sinclairs. I married her for her connections in the county and because I was given to understand that she had considerable expectations. You see, I am prepared to be perfectly frank with you. There is no reason for not being. You are quite capable of discovering for yourself that my wife is thirteen years older than I am and has no interests or, indeed, conversation beyond the technicalities of breeding West Highland terriers. Naturally you would begin to wonder why I, or any other man for that matter, ever married her. Well, I have told you. Unfortunately the money which I thought would accompany her was, in the first place, considerably less than gossip had claimed and, in the second place, it was not at my wife's disposal. Her uncle, Sir Quintin Sinclair, inherited not only the family title but virtually all the money as well. He was a bachelor, though, and enjoyed the most heartening ill-health. He was sixty-one at the time of my marriage and we were all hoping for his early decease when the money and the title would have passed to my wife's father. However, my father-in-law died and Sir Quintin is still with us. He made my wife and her cousin, Ottilia, his heirs. This meant that the inheritance, when we got it, would be half what it should have been. But worse was to come. Both Ottilia and my wife eventually gave birth to daughters and the old fool immediately changed his will and made these two grand-nieces his joint heirs. Shortly after this idiotic proceeding my wife and I agreed to separate. We had really only remained together for as long as we did out of deference to Sir Quintin. As a confirmed bachelor he had some very romantic views about marriage. In any case, by this time my need of liquid capital had been satisfied in other quarters. Money from my wife's family no longer had the least importance for me.'

Dover suppressed a yawn and blinked his eyes very rapidly in an attempt to stay awake. 'So your daughter has got some money of her own, then?'

Mr Wibbley stared at him disdainfully. 'No,' he replied with exaggerated patience. 'I thought I had already made it clear to you that she had not.'

'But this inheritance from Sir What's-his-name?'

'Sir Quintin is still with us. Or, at least, I presume he is. His housekeeper would have been certain to inform me if he had died. He has been completely gaga for many years and is the strongest argument I know of for compulsory euthanasia.'

Dover frowned dejectedly. Enough was enough! How much longer was this chatter going on? There was one thing about Wibbley – he certainly liked the sound of his own voice.

'Have you any more questions, Dover?'

Dover sighed. He'd plenty of questions, such as when was he going to be able to crawl into bed? Or, why don't you belt up? 'This Sir Quintin, Mr Wibbley, is he going to leave a lot of money?'

Mr Wibbley laughed shortly. 'Enough to cover his funeral expenses, I hope. Throughout their entire history the Sinclairs have lived up to and beyond their incomes. Sir Quintin has been no exception. I have no hesitation in admitting that marrying into that family was one of the few mistakes of my entire business career. My father warned me that they were a collection of whited sepulchres but, at the time, I thought I knew better. I have really no idea how much Sir Quintin will leave. Five or six thousand, perhaps? I doubt very much if it will be more. However, none of this has any bearing on my daughter's murder and, since that is now your chief concern, I shall not detain you any longer. I should like her husband charged with the murder as soon as possible but not before you have a cast-iron case against him. Should you wish any further information I shall be at your disposal at any hour of the day or night, but kindly ring my secretary first for an appointment.'

Dover rose laboriously and thankfully to his feet but Mr Wibbley had not quite finished with him.

'I was wondering, Dover, if perhaps, when this business has been cleared up, you might be able to help me on another matter. I am thinking of introducing a new position in my business – Director of Security. I shall be looking for a man who has had considerable police experience, at Scotland Yard, perhaps. I imagine the salary will be around four thousand pounds a year and there will be the usual perks, of course – a company house, a car – you know the sort of thing. You may be able to recommend a colleague, perhaps, who would be suitable? I make only one stipulation. He must be a man who carries out his duties successfully and one who would fulfil any wishes I might have to the letter. You – er – understand?'

A wink is as good as a nod. Dover emerged from the study, clutching his bowler hat and his overcoat and feeling somewhat overcome. Four thousand pounds a year and perks! He, Wilfred Dover, had actually been offered a bribe of four thousand pounds a year and perks! It was unbelievable!

MacGregor got up from a chair in the hall. 'Gosh, sir, you've been in there *hours*!'

Dover stared vacantly at him. And it had all been done so delicately. He was a real gentleman, Mr Wibbley was – when you got to know him. Dover was touched. There were few occasions in his career when he had been offered a bribe, and never one of such magnitude. Most criminals preferred to trust to his well-known incompetence and save their ill-gotten gains.

'You must be worn out, sir,' said MacGregor with an entirely self-orientated sympathy.

All he'd got to do, thought Dover gleefully, was shove Mr Wibbley's murderous son-in-law in the nick and then collect the jackpot. And he'd tell 'em a few home truths at the Yard when he handed in his resignation! They'd turn bright green with envy when they heard. He'd show 'em! All these years he'd been held back and passed over and trampled on – he'd show 'em! Thought he was a clapped-out old dead-beat, did they? Said he was bone idle and wouldn't recognize a clue if it was handed to him on a plate, did they? Well, he who laughs last, laughs longest. And with four thousand a year and a house and a car, Chief Inspector Wilfred Dover would be laughing so loud ...

'I expect he was very cut up about it, was he, sir?' Mac-Gregor was getting worried. The thought that some benign providence had struck his lord and master deaf and dumb was a heady one, but MacGregor rejected it. He knew his luck.

Still, the old fool was behaving in a most peculiar way. Mac-Gregor had expected him to come storming out of the study cursing like a trooper and demanding to be conveyed to his bed without delay.

'Sir ... ?' MacGregor began again.

Dover continued to stare straight through him. It was a just reward, really, for all those miserable years when he'd been forced to work for a living. Four thouand pounds *and* a house *and* a car! And for what? Just for running in the yobbo who'd done the murder in the first place. Well, he – Dover – had better get on with it. He didn't want to keep Mr Wibbley waiting, did he?

The blank, dazed look on Dover's face faded and was replaced by his habitual scowl. 'Wadderyersay?' he snarled.

MacGregor sighed. Things were getting back to normal. 'I was just wondering if Mr Wibbley was very upset about his daughter's death, sir.'

'Huh,' said Dover.

'Chief Inspector Bream's scared stiff of him, you know, sir. It seems he's practically God Almighty here in Pott Winckle. Oh, and by the way, sir, that Rolls and the chauffeur – it appears that Mr Wibbley has placed them at our disposal for the rest of our time here. I've got them standing by now.'

'So I should hope,' said Dover. 'Though, knowing you, it's a miracle that you haven't packed 'em off to the other end of the county.'

'Well, I thought you'd want to be getting to the hotel and snatching a bit of rest, sir,' said MacGregor, dutifully turning the other cheek. 'After all, you have been up all night, sir.'

Dover was well aware that he'd been up all night and, in normal circumstances, the investigation would have been shelved until he'd caught up with his sleep. But not *this* investigation! Oh dear me, no! 'What time is it?' he demanded.

'Just gone six, sir.'

For one craven moment Dover wondered if it was worth it.

'I've asked the hotel to lay on an early breakfast for us, sir, and your room's all ready for you.'

'Breakfast?' snapped Dover. 'We haven't time for breakfast. This is a murder case — or had you forgotten? We can't afford to waste a minute. I should have thought even you knew that.'

MacGregor did know it, only too well. In his experience it was always the Chief Inspector who insisted on dropping everything for his four hot meals a day and his twelve hours' uninterrupted sleep.

But, here was Dover already struggling into his overcoat. MacGregor rushed to help, having found that it didn't pay to let the old muddler over-exert himself. 'What exactly are we going to do then, sir?'

'We're going to visit the scene of the crime, you nit! What else?'

Number 17 Birdsfoot-Trefoil Close looked, in the grey light of dawn, depressingly like all the other forty-nine houses in the same road. Only the presence of a policeman, huddled up in his cape against the front door, singled it out from its more fortunate neighbours.

The policeman hesitated for a fraction of a second when he saw Dover approaching and appeared uncertain whether to reach for his truncheon or the brim of his helmet. The Rolls-Royce, however, and the quiet elegance of Sergeant Mac-Gregor reassured him. He saluted and sneezed.

'No stamina, these young coppers!' observed Dover with a sneer as he pushed his way into the house.

'The body's still in the front room, sir,' said the constable who had been standing out in the rain all night and felt aggrieved by Dover's remark.

Dover headed straight for the kitchen.

'First things first,' he said to MacGregor as he sat himself down at the table. 'Get the kettle on!'

'Do you think we should, sir?' asked MacGregor doubtfully. In any case he objected very strongly to being employed as a tea-boy. 'The fingerprint people haven't been in yet. We may be destroying evidence if we start handling things.'

'So we may,' agreed Dover with ominous amiability. 'Good thing you remembered that, laddie. You'd better keep your gloves on, hadn't you? And while you're about it you might have a root round in that fridge and see if you can rustle me up some bacon and eggs.'

While MacGregor ruined a new pair of pigskin gloves with his culinary efforts Dover told him as much as was politic of the lengthy conversation he had had with Daniel Wibbley.

MacGregor was not impressed. 'Oh, he's just being vindictive, don't you think, sir? I mean, he didn't want his daughter to marry Perking in the first place and so, when this happens, he naturally blames it on his son-in-law. It's understandable, I suppose, but he's no evidence to support his accusation, has he? What's Perking's motive, for instance?'

'Husbands don't need motives for scragging their wives,' mumbled Dover through a mouthful of bacon. 'It's an occupational hazard. Aren't we having any toast?'

MacGregor gritted his teeth and reached for the bread knife. 'From all accounts, sir, Perking and his wife were a very devoted couple.'

'Oh? And who's "all accounts" when they're at home?'

'Well, Chief Inspector Bream, sir.'

'Him? I wouldn't trust him to give me the time of day! Typical provincial flat-foot, that's all he is.'

'He may not be over-bright, sir, I admit, but he does know the town. He's lived in Pott Winckle all his life and I don't think there's much going on here that he doesn't get wind of.'

'Who's his candidate for the drop, then?'

MacGregor permitted himself a faintly reproving smile. 'I'm sure Chief Inspector Bream is far too conscientious a police officer, sir, to start pointing the finger at anybody before he's given all the evidence full consideration. He's the last man to jump to hasty conclusions.'

Dover blew unpleasantly down his nose. 'Here, have you put marge on this toast?'

'I had a long chat with Chief Inspector Bream, sir, while I

31

was waiting for you. He gave me quite a bit of useful background material. You see, sir, assuming that this murder isn't just the work of some homicidal maniac, whoever killed Cynthia Perking must have had some reason for doing it, mustn't they, sir?'

'Her husband,' said Dover pushing his plate away from him and licking the marmalade off his fingers. 'He probably just got sick of her stupid face. You do, you know,' he added moodily. 'Got a fag, laddie?'

MacGregor took out his cigarette case. 'Yes, her husband is a possibility, sir, but he's not the only one. There's her cousin, for example.'

'Oh yes?' said Dover and handed his cup over for some more tea. 'And let's have a bit more sugar this time, laddie.'

'Her cousin's a man called Hereward Topping-Wibbley, sir, who ... '

'I don't believe it,' said Dover.

'You don't believe what, sir?'

'That name. Hereward Topping-Wibbley? Somebody's been pulling your leg, laddie.'

'I don't think so, sir. That actually is his name, I do assure you. His mother is Daniel Wibbley's sister. She married a man called Topping and, since the Wibbley family is so important round here, she had their name changed to Topping-Wibbley. Now, her son, Hereward—he's an only child, by the way—he's been brought up in the business. Everybody assumes that he'll take over the running of Wibbley Ware when Mr Wibbley retires or dies. But, of course, he won't have complete control. All Daniel Wibbley's shares would naturally be inherited by his daughter, and he's reputed to hold a pretty hefty majority. But you see the position, don't you, sir? With Cynthia Perking out of the way her cousin, Hereward, will be the sole heir. He'll come in for the lot. Now, that's what I call a motive.'

'Do you?' Dover gazed abstractedly at the ceiling. 'Got any more long-shot suspects up your sleeve? Because, if you have, you'd better spit 'em out now before we get down to the real work.'

'Well, sir,' said MacGregor hotly, 'there's Hereward Topping-Wibbley's mother, or his wife – either of them might have done it on his behalf.'

Dover rolled his eyes.

'Or there's Daniel Wibbley himself, sir.'

'What?' yelped Dover, leaping instantly to the defence of his patron-to-be. 'Kill his own daughter? You must be out of your pin-head mind!'

'They were estranged, sir, and they'd had plenty of blazing rows – everybody in Pott Winckle knows that. Daniel Wibbley was absolutely livid with fury over the marriage. It's common gossip that he'd tried to bribe young Perking to clear off and leave the girl alone. And having her and her low-class husband living in his town – he was furious about it.'

'A father's natural concern for his daughter's welfare!' bellowed Dover. 'It was his blasted son-in-law he couldn't stand the sight of!'

'That's as maybe, sir,' said MacGregor, still gallantly sticking to his guns, 'but Daniel Wibbley is used to having his own way and anybody who stands out against him gets pretty short shrift, from what I hear. And he's none too particular about the methods he uses, either. There's a pretty nasty rumour going round about how he forced his own father, when he was on his death bed, to sign a will making him sole heir to the business. The old man intended to split it between your Daniel Wibbley and his sister, Hereward's mother, but your Daniel Wibbley wasn't having any. He wanted the lot. Why, he's got the reputation of being the most ruthless businessman this side of the Wash! He could have come here yesterday afternoon, had yet another row with his daughter, lost his temper and killed her. It wouldn't be the first time he'd raised a hand to her, either. Chief Inspector Bream says … '

'I don't give a brass monkey what Chief Inspector blasted Bream said!' screamed Dover. 'I've never heard such a load of poppycock and old wives' tales in all my born days! Call yourself a detective? You're nothing but a lazy, malicious muck-raker! Here you are, jumping to conclusions like a cat on hot bricks before we've even seen the blooming body. Why, for all you know, it might bloody well be suicide!'

'I'm sorry, sir,' said MacGregor stiffly.

'And so you damned well should be,' retorted Dover, totally unappeased and still smarting at the injustice of MacGregor's insinuations. 'Going round, spouting out actionable slander like a ... ' Dover's lowly brow creased in thought. Like a what? He changed the subject. 'Is there any more tea in that pot?'

Meekly MacGregor shook his head. 'No, sir.'

'Right!' Dover hauled himself to his feet. 'In that case we might as well go and see the flaming corpse.'

Chapter Three

CYNTHIA PERKING, née Wibbley, had come to a sticky end all right, and in the literal meaning of the phrase. She lay huddled up by the fireplace in the front room, her head and shoulders an ugly mass of dark congealed blood.

"Strewth!" said Dover. 'What a way to go!'

'It looks like a straightforward murderous attack, doesn't it, sir?' MacGregor suggested tentatively. 'I mean — the clothing and everything. It doesn't look as though there'd been any attempt at sexual interference, does it? Still, the post mortem should be able to give us something definite on that.'

Dover moved over to the hearth. 'This the murder weapon?'

'That poker, sir? It seems likely. The lab'll be able to tell us for sure when they examine it, but those look like traces of blood and hair on it to me.'

Dover stared moodily round the room. 'Well, that disposes of the chance-intruder theory, doesn't it? It must have been somebody who knew there was a poker in here — and who better than her husband?'

This was too blatant for MacGregor, even in his rather chastened mood, to stomach. 'Oh, I don't think you can quite say that, sir,' he objected. 'Suppose it was a thief, say, who broke into the house? Mrs Perking catches him and he just picks up the nearest available weapon. Besides, anybody could guess that there'd more than likely be a poker in this room.'

'How?'

'Well, the coal fire, sir.'

'And how would they know there was a coal fire in here, Sergeant Clever-Devil?'

'They'd be able to see the smoke from the chimney, sir.'

Dover scowled ferociously. If there was one thing he couldn't stand it was people trying to take the mickey out of him. 'Anyhow, I can't see any villain worth his salt breaking into a dump like this in the middle of the day and with somebody actually in the place. What was he going to steal, for God's sake?'

MacGregor nodded. 'You've got a point there, sir,' he admitted. 'Still, even villains make mistakes, sometimes.'

Dover sniffed contemptuously. 'Any sign of breaking in?'

'Well, not the front door, sir, nor the back. And these windows here haven't been forced. And neither had the ones in the kitchen.'

'And how the blazes do you know?'

'I looked, sir. Just an automatic routine check.'

Dover's scowl grew blacker. 'What about the rest of the house?'

'I'm afraid we won't know about that until it's been examined, sir. You may remember that the local police were most meticulous about not touching a thing until we got here.'

'Somebody may just have walked in,' admitted Dover reluctantly. 'You know what some of these dratted housewives are like—don't lock their blooming doors or leave the key under the mat where anybody can get hold of it.'

'Well, that's possible, sir, but this house has got Yale locks both back and front. I imagine both doors would be kept locked because there doesn't appear to be any other means of keeping them shut. It seems a bit inadequate, but that's how they build these cheap houses nowadays. I should guess that it means that either Mrs Perking let her murderer into the house, or that he let himself in with a key.'

'Which means the husband,' said Dover with gloomy triumph. 'Told you he was the one.'

MacGregor was past arguing. He'd been up all night, too. 'Is there anything else you want to see in this room, sir? If not, I'll ring the local police and get them to send the fingerprint boys in, and the photographers. I suppose they can take the body away, too?'

Dover nodded. 'Might as well.'

'I'll just have a word with the chap outside. He can go and phone from the call box for me.'

MacGregor went out but in a few moments he came back again, accompanied by the dripping policeman.

'Excuse me, sir, but the constable here has a small piece of information.'

'That's right, sir,' said the policeman eagerly. 'P.C. Roberts, he's a mate of mine, see. He's on the cars and he was the one that come to the house when Mr Perking phoned up and said what had happened. He came into this room, Roberts did. Well, he had to, didn't he? I know Mr Perking said his wife had been murdered but you can't believe everything the general public tells you, can you, sir? Make our job a sight easier if you could, eh? Well, sir, as I was saying, P.C. Roberts is a mate of mine and he was telling me all about it down at the nick before I come on duty. White as a sheet he was, sir, even then. And he'd been sick, too. Never seen a dead body before, Roberts hadn't. Well, not a murdered one, anyhow. Come to think of it, sir,' – the policeman gulped – 'neither have I. Not till now, that is. It's horrible, sarge, isn't it?' He turned appealingly to MacGregor.

MacGregor was unsympathetic. 'Get on with it, man!' he hissed. 'The Chief Inspector hasn't got all day to listen to your ramblings.'

'Oh yes, sir! Sorry, sir! Well, sir, what struck my mate was that it all looked so homely, sir. There was this nice blazing fire in the grate and the telly was still on. Real gruesome it was, Roberts said. This young woman lying here in a pool of blood and some joker on the telly yacking away about productivity or suchlike.'

Dover looked bleakly at MacGregor and MacGregor looked bleakly at the chrysanthemum-patterned wallpaper.

'Is that it?' asked Dover.

'I thought the fact that the deceased had been watching television might be important, sir.' MacGregor, to his fury, could feel a blush spreading up over his face.

'Did you?'

'Er – yes, sir.'

'If anybody wants me,' said Dover, 'I'll be in the kitchen.'

It was nearly an hour before MacGregor was free to join him. He found Dover fast asleep in a wicker chair with his feet up on the draining board. He let MacGregor cough his throat sore before he consented to open his eyes.

'Everything's under control, sir,' MacGregor reported happily. 'The body's been removed and the fingerprint men are nearly through. There's no sign of anybody breaking in, sir, by the way. We've checked the whole house. I was wondering if you wanted to see Perking himself now, sir? He's spent the night at his sister's, apparently, and I was wondering whether you wanted to interview him there or have him brought back here.'

Dover yawned, removed his feet from the draining board and rubbed the back of his thick policeman's neck. 'No,' he said at last.

'Er – no what, sir?'

'I don't want to see him yet. What's the matter with you – got cloth ears or something?'

'But he found the body, sir.' MacGregor didn't relish the task of trying to teach the Chief Inspector his job, but somebody had to. 'He'll be able to tell us if any of the doors were open or if there was … '

'Later,' rumbled Dover.

'But he's a basic witness, sir. He's not made a statement yet. He's not even been interviewed.'

'He'll keep,' said Dover. He got up and wandered aimlessly over to a cupboard and opened it.

MacGregor squirmed. 'Sir,' he pointed out, 'nobody's checked this room for fingerprints yet. You may, quite unwittingly of course, be accidentally destroying evidence.'

Dover picked up a packet off the shelf. It was a wonder cake-mix. Solemnly and with the sole purpose of annoying MacGregor he read laboriously through the instructions. All you needed to add was two eggs, sugar, butter and vanilla extract. Dover tossed the packet back in the cupboard with a snort of disgust. 'Wonder cake-mix, my Aunt Fannie!' he exploded, well aware that his sergeant was hanging on his every word. 'They used to call it flour in my day!'

MacGregor was on the rack. Sometimes – not often, but sometimes – when the Chief Inspector's behaviour plumbed the very depths of childishness and irresponsibility, the old fool was actually pursuing a profitable line of investigation. It meant that one couldn't be too careful. The last thing MacGregor's self-esteem could tolerate was Dover stealing a march on him.

Dover, whistling tunelessly and nonchalantly, continued to poke around. He helped himself to a couple of biscuits out of a tin. He examined the contents of the fridge. He placed his heavily booted foot on the pedal of the yellow plastic pedal bin and, thoughtfully wrinkling his nose, inspected the contents thereof. He opened a selection of the available drawers and, in the end, was reduced to gravely turning the taps on and off over the sink.

A knock on the door leading into the hall saved him from further exertion. MacGregor went to open it. There was a short murmured conversation and MacGregor came back.

'Excuse me, sir, that was the fingerprint boys. They'd like to move in here, if' – MacGregor made the pause as insubordinate as he dared – 'you've quite finished.'

Dover pulled out a handkerchief which had given much sterling service since it was last washed and blew his nose.

'Sir?'

'Oh, let 'em in! There's no peace for the wicked. We'll go and interview the neighbours. They may have seen something.'

Dover wandered off and, led by an unfailing instinct in these matters, struck it lucky the first time off. Young Mrs Carruthers next door was just making herself a cup of coffee after the usual morning upheaval of getting her husband off to work. Mrs Carruthers was harassed – with eight children under five milling around her this was not surprising – but she was hospitable. She offered the two detectives a cup of coffee in their turn and

39

brushed aside MacGregor's polite protests with a jocund laugh and the assurance that there was plenty more instant in the tin.

Dover cleared a space for himself, unceremoniously dumping piles of nappies, toys, dirty bibs and a large hammer on to the floor, and prepared to listen. Once Mrs Carruthers had established the identity of her early-morning callers she needed little further stimulus.

'Oh yes, we've heard what happened all right. Dreadful, isn't it? And right next door, too. My brother once knew a fellow who committed suicide but I've never been mixed up in anything like this before. It's awful, isn't it? They do say her head was beaten in something terrible—brains splashed all round the walls so somebody told my hubbie in the pub last night. Shocking, isn't it? Poor girl!' She grabbed a passing infant, hoisted its knickers up for it and sent it on its way with a resounding slap on its bottom without pausing for more than the shortest of breaths. 'And, of course, as I said to my hubbie, it's only natural that I should be more upset than the other ladies in the road. I mean, we were quite good pals. My hubbie didn't like that, you know—me calling her Cynthia and her calling me Elsie. It's his job, you see. He works at Wibbley's and naturally he didn't want to get on the wrong side of Mr Wibbley. Well, you can understand that, can't you? He said he didn't want to get mixed up in the family's private affairs and I said, well you're not, are you? And he said, no, but you are and we had quite a row about it. But I didn't let it make any difference. I take people as I find them, I do. I always have and I always will and I got on all right with Cynthia. She was a damned sight better company than some of the other old cats living on this estate, that I can tell you. And, as I said to my hubbie, the trouble with you is, I said, you're like all the rest of them. You can't see further than the nose on your face. All right, I said, so she's quarrelled with her father and he's cut her off with the proverbial shilling so you and all the other people who work at Wibbley's shun her as though she's got the proverbial plague. But Mr Wibbley isn't going to live for ever, is he, I said. One day he'll pass on and who'll own

Wibbley's then, I asked. My friend Cynthia will, I said, and maybe she'll remember them that passed the time of day with her when she was down on her luck. And maybe she won't, he said. He's one of that sort, you know. There's no arguing with him. Marleen! Put that down, darling, it's too heavy for you and … Well, I did tell you, didn't I, darling? Never mind, I'll clean it up later. You can't keep the place decent two minutes together with kids around so you might just as well learn to live with it. Of course I was half joking, really. About Cynthia, I mean. I quite liked her and she was always all right with me. No side or anything, you know. Didn't try to make you feel inferior like most of the old cats round here do. Talk about keeping up with the Joneses – believe me, that *started* in Birdsfoot-Trefoil Close! No, funnily enough, it was the other way round, really. Well, I mean, he couldn't have been bringing home more than about twelve quid a week from that travel agency and she'd about as much idea of managing as flying to the moon. Extravagant? You wouldn't believe some of the things she used to throw her money away on when she first came here. And as for cooking – well, she all but needed a recipe book to boil an egg with at the beginning. That's really how we started to get friendly, you see. We used to say good morning, over-the-garden-wall stuff, you know, and then she got to asking my advice about bits of things and before you knew where you were she was popping in here most mornings for a cup of coffee and a bit of a chat. Mind you, she'd do a bit of shopping for me to save me going out and things like that, so there was benefits on both sides. Well, at first we used to talk about cooking and washing and all that sort of thing and what we'd seen on the telly the night before. She was a terror for the telly, she really was! Some of these serial things she used to watch real religiously. She wouldn't miss them for anything. Of course, they hardly ever went out at all – couldn't really afford it, poor things – and when you haven't got a pack of kids under your feet all day you can whip through your housework in no time. And, of course, that was the next thing she started asking my advice about: kids. John-Paul! Give that hat back to the kind gentleman, there's a good boy! Go on, give it back this minute! Hurry up, I shan't tell you again, John-Paul! Oh well, yes — it would be better if you kept it on your knees, p'raps. He hasn't damaged it, has he? Oh? Well, that'll straighten out all right, I expect. And just stop making that row, John-Paul, and go and play with your sister. He's got a thing about hats, that kid has. And bowler hats he just can't resist. The never-never man came round last week and while I was getting the money he gave John-Paul his bowler to play with. Ever such a kind man, he is, and very fond of kiddies. Well, I should hate to tell you what John-Paul did! Quick as a flash he was. Of course, I felt awful but, really, I could hardly keep a straight face. Of course, this chap couldn't see the funny side of it but he was very nice about it. I had to offer to pay for his hat and everything but he said not to bother, accidents would happen. I don't know about accidents. If you ask me, John-Paul did it deliberate. Anyhow, I'm always extra careful when anybody comes in with a bowler hat now. Well, as I was saying, Cynthia didn't start worrying until they'd been married a year and there wasn't a sign of anything. Well, at first I kept saying the usual things, like you do. Telling her to relax and forget about it, but every month she used to come in here with a face as long as a fiddle and I'd know we were back to square one again. And, of course, it got to be more than just wanting a baby. There was her father, you see. It seems he'd said some pretty rotten things about John Per- king when there was all the trouble before she married him, sort of casting reflections on his manhood, if you know what I mean. Well, I know John Perking does look a bit of a weed but there was no call for Mr Wibbley to cast aspersions like that. I mean, who's he to talk when he's at home? They only ever had Cynthia and one kid hardly constitutes a world record, does it? Well, of course, Cynthia was just longing for the day when she could go waltzing along to her father and spit in his eye and tell him she was pregnant. It got to be the only thing she cared about. It'd prove her husband was just as good as anybody else and I think she'd a pretty good idea her father would be only too pleased to forgive and forget if he had a grandson. And she didn't like living here, you know, not really. She put up with it, of course, and I don't mean she didn't love her husband but—well—this wasn't her kind of life and it's no good pretending it was. But she could only get out of it by having a baby. Of course, I suppose if she'd left her husband her father would have taken her back all right, but I'm sure the idea never crossed her mind. After all, she'd got her pride, hadn't she? They were absolutely devoted to each other—a bit too sloppy, if you ask me, but then it wouldn't do for us all to be the same, would it? Well, sloppy or not, it didn't produce any results. She used to come in here, Cynthia did, and sit just where you're sitting at this very table and ask me what to do. As if I was an expert! I mean, I have 'em like shelling peas, once a year regular as clockwork and no damned pill on the market makes the slightest bit of difference. I tell you, round here they call this house The Warren! All these kids aren't mine, by the way. I'm just baby-sitting one or two for the lady on the other side. After all, eight are no more trouble than four, are they, really? Well, some of the conversations Cynthia and me had round this very table would make your hair curl, really they would! My husband used to say it was downright disgusting and an invasion of a man's privacy but, like I said, how can I help if I don't know what they're doing? Well, it went on and on and in the end Cynthia goes, on the q.t., mind you—to the doctor. Well, to cut a long story short, he said there was nothing wrong with *her*. So you can see where that left us, can't you? Only, of course, Cynthia didn't feel as though she could ask him. She thought if it turned out to be his fault really he'd be completely shattered and she just couldn't bring herself to do that to him. I kept telling her it might just be something that the doctor could put right and she kept saying, but supposing it isn't, and bursting into tears. Oh, we had some real old how-do-you-do's, I don't mind telling you, but she wouldn't budge. She just preferred to let him go on thinking that it was all her fault that they couldn't start a baby. I suppose it was all very noble and

43

touching and what have you, but at times I really did feel like giving her a good shake. It was just like one of those daft plays on the telly where if somebody would only use a bit of common sense they wouldn't get in to all these messes. Oh, that clock's five minutes fast, by the way. I checked it by the pips this morning. Well, you can imagine my surprise when a couple of months ago Cynthia comes bursting in here looking like she'd come up on the Pools. I've never seen her so excited. Mind you, as soon as I realized *that* was all she was going on, I tried to calm her down a bit. Like I told her, just missing a month doesn't mean a thing. There might be a hundred reasons for it. But she just laughed and called me a wet blanket. She was certain she was pregnant and nothing me or anybody else might say would make a blooming bit of difference. Well, I asked her what Mr Perking had had to say about it and she said she hadn't told him, just in case. She was going to wait till she was absolutely, one hundred per cent certain and then break the good news. So, she had got *some* common sense, hadn't she? Well, a month went by and I was nearly having kittens myself, half expecting her to come in here one morning and say that the worst had happened and it was all a false alarm. But the days kept going by and in the end even I had to admit that she was probably right and she'd really clicked this time. Well, it was then she decided that she couldn't wait any longer. She was going to go to the doctor and get it absolutely definite from him that she was pregnant. So, one day last week, off she goes – still not saying a word to her hubbie, of course. Well, of course, two months gone is pretty early so the doctor had to take a blood test or something. Cynthia did tell me, something to do with rabbits, I think. So, that meant another wait until the results came through. Well, they came through yesterday morning. They were positive and, believe me, that poor girl was just about taking off with excitement. After three years she'd finally made it! Well, of course, she just couldn't wait to tell her old man the good news. She made a point of never phoning him up at the office – he didn't like it, seemingly – but on this occasion she was going to make an exception. And

44

that was the last time I saw her alive, poor thing, when she walked out of my kitchen to go and telephone her husband. And then this rotten thing had to happen to her! Just when she was so happy … '

Young Mrs Carruthers's voice faltered and she brushed the tears from her eyes with the back of her hand. The kitchen suddenly seemed very quiet. MacGregor glanced at Dover to see if he was prepared to put the necessary questions. From the look on his face, he apparently wasn't. MacGregor was gratified. This meant that the burden of the interrogation would fall on his younger and more capable shoulders and the investigation now stood a good chance of taking a decisive step forward.

'What you're saying, Mrs Carruthers, is that Mrs Perking was pregnant?'

Mrs Carruthers, who was about to blow her nose on her handkerchief, paused and looked at MacGregor in some amazement. She was under the impression that she had made the situation crystal-clear. 'Yes,' she said.

MacGregor treated her to a patronizing smile. 'It's just to get the record quite straight,' he assured her. 'And her husband knew of her condition?'

'Well, I suppose so. I didn't actually hear her tell him, if that's what you mean. No, Albertina! Leave Auntie's coffee cup alone, there's a good girl! No, now don't do that, darling! Oh, you naughty girl — just look what a mess you've made all over the table!' Mrs Carruthers sighed and smiled wanly at MacGregor. 'Thank God for plastic tablecloths, eh? It just run straight off. Oh, has it gone on your trousers? It's funny but I've noticed it before, that table does seem to slope that way. There's a dishcloth in the sink if you'd like to mop yourself up a bit. There, Albertina, you see what you've done now, don't you? Just you say you're sorry or this nice gentleman'll come along and lock you up in a cell and you won't like that, will you?'

While MacGregor tried to forestall the total ruin of a pair of very expensive trousers, Dover creaked into some semblance of life. A couple of trusting infants were attempting to climb up on to his knees. Dover detached them with alacrity and, as they retreated bawling into a corner, he turned to Mrs Carruthers.

'You were in here all yesterday afternoon, were you?'

'Well, me and the kids, that is,' agreed Mrs Carruthers, eyeing Dover uneasily.

'Did you go over to the Perking's house at all yesterday?'

'No, of course, I didn't. It was Cynthia who always came in here to see me. I can't leave the kids, can I? If you turn your back for one minute the little devils have this place torn apart.'

Dover stared gloomily at her. 'So, if a witness said she saw you going into the Perking's house at five o'clock yesterday afternoon, she'd be lying, would she?'

'She certainly would!' Young Mrs Carruthers went very red in the face. 'I was in this very kitchen all afternoon and I never left the house for one single moment.'

'Can you prove it?'

'Well, no — of course I can't prove it!' spluttered Mrs Carruthers. 'Here, what are you getting at?'

'And if a witness said she saw you coming out of the Perking's house at a quarter to six, that'd be another lie would it?'

'It definitely would!' Mrs Carruthers's eyes narrowed. 'It's that Hutchinson bitch, isn't it?' she asked angrily. 'Her right opposite, across the back lane? The rotten old cow! She's nothing but a wicked old trouble-maker, that's all she is. Right, well she's met her match this time! You two can just stop here for a couple of minutes and keep an eye on the kids while I go across and deal with old mother Hutchinson once and for all! Only, this time, I'll black both her bleeding eyes!'

Chapter Four

MacGregor turned away from the sink and stared at Dover in incredulous and mute reproach. Upstairs Mrs Carruthers could be heard muttering to herself as she crashed around in search of a hat suitable for the doing of Mrs Hutchinson. In the kitchen, once the initial shock had worn off, the infants set up an ear-splitting yowl of deprivation.

MacGregor forgot about his ruined trousers. 'Sir, how *could* you?' he reproached his Chief Inspector. 'There isn't a witness, is there? You haven't taken a statement from anybody! You can't have done. You ... '

'There's no need to take a knife and fork to it!' growled Dover. 'Besides, I never said there was a witness, did I? I just asked her what she'd say *if*. It was a purely hypothetical question.'

'A hypothetical question?' repeated MacGregor, only just stopping his voice rising to a shriek which would have beaten the infants at their own game. 'But what on earth did you want to go putting a hypothetical question like that for?'

'Here,' said Dover, a great one for sitting on his dignity, 'I'll thank you to remember who you're talking to, laddie! We aren't running a democracy round here and don't you forget it.'

MacGregor gritted his teeth. 'I'm sorry, sir,' he said tightly. 'It's just that I was wondering if you had any ulterior motive, of which I am unfortunately unaware, for putting such a hypothetical question to Mrs Carruthers.'

'She yacks too much,' muttered Dover sullenly. 'Talk about a never-ending stream! And don't you start coming the sarky with me, either, laddie! She needed teaching a lesson. You'd think we'd nothing else to do all day except sit around on our backsides listening to her gabbling her stupid head off.'

47

'Well, that's really what a large part of our job consists of, isn't it, sir?' ventured MacGregor carefully. 'It gets very boring at times, I do admit, but it's a cross we have to bear.'

'Oh, I can quite believe it doesn't bother you,' said Dover nastily. 'You'd spend your whole life lolling about doing nothing if you were given half the chance. Well, it doesn't do for me, laddie. I like a bit of action myself.'

MacGregor raised his eyes to the ceiling. 'It sounds as though you've got it, sir.'

Dover sniggered. 'I was wondering how she'd take it. She's a very neurotic type, if you ask me.' He scratched his unshaven chin reflectively. 'Here, you don't think by any chance that I've scored a bull's eye, do you, laddie?'

'No, sir, I don't,' MacGregor replied resolutely. Things, in his opinion, had already gone quite far enough.

'Oh, I wouldn't be too sure. Very guilty reaction that was, if you ask me. I mean, if she didn't go into next door yesterday afternoon, what does she want to go flying off the handle like that for, eh?'

'I'm sure I don't know, sir, but, since by the sound of it, Mrs Carruthers is coming downstairs you'll be able to ask her yourself.'

But MacGregor wasn't going to be allowed to get away with it as easily as that. To his lot fell the task of assuaging the understandably outraged sensibilities of young Mrs Carruthers. Not surprisingly she found it difficult to comprehend that she had been the victim of a light-hearted joke. Looking dazed, she sat down at the kitchen table and clutched a selection of infants to her bosom. 'I've come over all shaky,' she said resentfully, pushing her best hat back off her brow. 'My knees have gone as weak as water, they have really.'

'Why don't you make us all a nice cup of tea?' asked Dover helpfully.

Young Mrs Carruthers shook her head and laid her collapsible umbrella on the table. It fell heavily. Mrs Hutchinson was never to know how lucky she'd been. 'I shall have to go and apologize to her first, shan't I?' asked Mrs Carruthers piteously. 'I mean, the things I was saying about her. She'll never let me hear the last of it. That other row we had – that was bad enough. But, this time ... '

'Oh, for goodness' sake, pull yourself together, woman!' Dover's paper-thin patience was fraying at the edges. 'Mrs Whatever-her-name-is doesn't know what you've been saying about her, so you've nothing to worry about, have you?'

'Ah,' said Mrs Carruthers in gloomy triumph, 'but she'll guess, won't she? She knows me. She knows I wouldn't sit quietly twiddling my thumbs while people were casting aspersions on my good name and all but accusing me of murdering my best friend.'

'But she hasn't cast any bloody aspersions!' raged Dover, his thirst getting the better of him. 'I haven't even spoken to the blasted woman! I've never even laid eyes on her and she's never accused you of anything.'

'Oh yes, she has! Indeed she has! What about that time her scruffy old cat went missing? With all these rowdy teenagers hanging about the place, who does she have to pick on? My poor little ... '

'MacGregor!' Dover brought a truly baleful glance to bear on his subordinate. 'I'm not going to stand much more of this. Get this woman calmed down and be quick about it!'

Eventually MacGregor, employing all his tact and boyish charm at full strength, got Mrs Carruthers back to as near normal as she was likely to be for some considerable time. She'd had a bad shock and, as she herself put it, it would be ages before she got back her trust in human nature. However, she incarcerated most of the infants behind bars in a stout play pen and set about making a cup of tea for the adults.

Dover grabbed a handful of rusks and bravely pressed the button which would set Mrs Carruthers off again. 'Did you see anything out of the ordinary going on next door yesterday afternoon?'

Young Mrs Carruthers stopped stirring her tea. 'Round at Cynthia's? Well now, it's funny you should ask me that,

49

because I didn't. I mean, when your next-door neighbour gets murdered, you'd think you'd see something, wouldn't you? Well, I've been racking my brains ever since I heard what happened but I can't call to mind a thing that struck me as being odd. Of course, unlike some I could name, I don't spend all my time gawping out of the window, spying on what my neighbours are doing. If you want a minute by minute account of what happened at Number 17 I suggest you go and ask your friend Mrs Hutchinson.'

Dover scowled and MacGregor leapt in with a question.

'What time did Mrs Perking leave you yesterday?'

'Well now, I suppose it'd be about half past twelve. I know it was getting quite late because, of course, she'd had to wait simply ages at the doctor's. He's always busy, he is. Of course he's supposed to be very good but, as I told my hubbie, you need all your health and strength to sit it out in his dratted waiting room until it's your turn.'

'And you didn't see Cynthia Perking again after she left here?'

'No, I didn't. Mind you, that would have been unusual if I had done, because it was mornings when she used to pop in here.'

'Did her husband come home to lunch?'

'Oh, no. They do a lot of their business at the travel agency with people calling in in their dinner hour, so he generally used to take sandwiches and eat 'em whenever he got a spare moment. So Cynthia was like me, she just used to have a snack lunch because you don't want to go cooking twice, do you? Of course, I've got the kids to cope with but now you can get all these tins it makes life a lot easier, doesn't it? I used to say to Cynthia she didn't know when she was well off. You won't be able to sit watching telly with your feet up all afternoon, I used to tell her, not when you've got a baby to look after, you won't, I said. Because that's just about all she did, you know. She got all her housework done in the morning and all her shopping and then she'd have a bit of lunch and then she'd be off, straight into that front room of theirs and on with

50

the telly. And there she'd sit until a quarter to six. She always watched that serial thing, you know. Oh, what's it called? You know—the one that's set in that marriage advice bureau place? *For Better or Worse*—that's what it's called. I've watched it once or twice myself and a bigger load of rubbish I've never seen in all my born days. Still, Cynthia was mad about it and she wouldn't miss it for anything. Soon as it was over she'd switch off and dash into the kitchen and start getting the supper ready. Her husband got home about ten past six, you see, so it just about gave her time. As far as I could make out she used to stick practically everything under the grill and that doesn't take long, does it? No wonder she couldn't make her housekeeping last beyond Wednesday. Why don't you make a stew, I said, or a shepherd's pie or something.'

MacGregor was writing furiously in his notebook. 'Just a minute, Mrs Carruthers, let me see if I've got this straight. Mrs Perking sat in the front room until a quarter to six. After a quarter to six she'd be in the kitchen getting dinner ready for her husband who would get home from work at approximately ten minutes past six. Is that right?'

'Yes. Well, that's what usually happened. And yesterday, well, I'd no reason to think that everything wasn't going on just as usual. I was upstairs putting some of the kids to bed— my hubbie can't stand 'em crawling all over him when he's had a hard day at work so I try to get 'em out of the way before he comes home. Well, I was upstairs in the back bedroom and I happened to look out of the window and I saw Mr Perking bicycling up the lane, just like any other day.'

'What time was this?' asked MacGregor eagerly, his pencil poised.

'Oh, round about ten past six, same as usual. You could almost set your watch by him. I remember thinking he didn't look 'specially excited or anything. He put his bike away in the shed and locked it up after him and took his bicycle clips off, just as though it was any ordinary day. I tell you, I felt like belting downstairs and giving him a damned good shaking. I mean, he'd just heard he was going to be a father after three years' trying and he couldn't even manage to get home a bit earlier—never mind bring his wife a bunch of flowers or something. Oh, these men—they really make you sick sometimes.'

'But you don't know for sure that Mrs Perking had told him about the baby, do you?'

Mrs Carruthers shrugged her shoulders. 'Oh well, if you're going to try and make excuses for him ... '

'Did you see anything else?'

'No. He went in at the back door and that was that. I didn't hear what had happened—the murder, I mean—until my hubbie came in later that night from the pub. He picks up all the gossip there.'

MacGregor studied his notebook with suppressed excitement. He checked over the times and movements to himself, just to make perfectly sure. Yes, it was all there.

'Sir,' he began.

Dover reluctantly opened his eyes. 'Uh?'

'I think we've just about got all the information Mrs Carruthers has at the moment, sir. I expect she'd be glad to see the back of us and get on with the housework and everything.'

'Oh, you needn't bother about me,' Mrs Carruthers chipped in comfortably. 'The housework can just go hang today. I'm far too upset to bother with things like that.'

Chief Inspector Dover relaxed visibly. It was warm and cosy in the kitchen and he'd got used to the smell of the infants. He gave Mrs Carruthers an encouraging smile and passed his cup over. 'Bit more milk this time, there's a good girl.'

MacGregor regard this touching little domestic scene with irritation. 'I really think we ought to be making a move, sir. I've got one or two points I'd like to discuss with you and they are—well—rather confidential.'

Dover was relieved of the effort of wriggling out of this one by a solid knocking on the back door.

'It's not locked!' trilled Mrs Carruthers.

The policeman who had been on guard duty at the scene of

the crime poked his head round the door. Such infants as were old enough to recognize a police uniform screamed and panicked in their playpen.

'Sorry to intrude, missus, but are them detectives still here? Oh, there you are, sir.' He stepped gingerly over the threshold and pulled the door to behind him. 'It's a Mrs Withycombe, sir,' He removed his helmet with a sigh of relief. 'She come across to me just now when I was *still* on duty outside the front door and said she'd got some evidence. I tried to get her to make a statement to one of the C.I.D. men what's swarming all over the house in there, but it's you she insists on seeing. Even knew your name and rank, sir. Beats me how they do it. Never move from their own front parlours, some of 'em don't, and yet they've only got to see you walking down the street and they've got it all off pat. They know more about you than your own mother does. Well now, sir, and what do you want me to do about this Mrs Withycombe, sir?'

Dover regarded the police constable sourly. 'Where is the old hag?'

'She's right outside that door, sir,' replied the constable loudly. 'And, if I'm any judge of character, she'll have her ear all but glued to that keyhole!' He winked broadly at Dover. Dover scowled back at him, not approving of fraternization with the lower ranks. 'Wheel her in!' he growled.

Mrs Withycombe entered the kitchen as though penetrating a den of lions. Her eyes flicked rapidly round the room, accurately registering the location, condition, make and estimated H.P. cost of every piece of kitchen equipment.

Mrs Carruthers bridled instinctively and pushed her tea cup over the stained patch on the table. 'Oh, it's you, is it?' she remarked with a distinct lack of hospitality.

Mrs Withycombe smiled from a great distance. 'Pleased to meet you, I'm sure.' Her glance went darting off again. 'I've often seen you knocking about of course.'

'I'll bet you have!' Mrs Carruthers turned to Dover. 'We've lived in the same road', she informed him, somewhat to his surprise, 'for six years and, to the best of my knowledge, it's

53

the first time we've ever spoken. Very neighbourly round here they are.'

'We like to keep ourselves to ourselves at our house,' said Mrs Withycombe primly. 'I wouldn't have dreamed of intruding now, but I thought it was my duty to tell the police what I know.' She smoothed her white cotton gloves on her hands. Thus drawing attention to the fact that she was wearing them.

Young Mrs Carruthers seethed. 'Well, you'd better take a seat then. Unless, that is, you think you might get your best coat dirty.' She nodded at a vacant chair.

Mrs Withycombe forgave her with a thin smile and perched herself on the edge of the seat. She cleared her throat, politely raising her gloved hand to her mouth as she did so. The infants watched her with great interest. 'It's the first time I've been in somebody else's house on the estate,' she told Dover in a lady-like whisper. 'Mr Withycombe and I, we don't believe in intruding.' She looked round the kitchen again. 'It must be just the same as ours, I suppose, but somehow it looks quite different.'

'Not so clean, I suppose?' challenged Mrs Carruthers pugnaciously.

'Well, not quite so tidy, shall we say,' said Mrs Withycombe with another of her smug little smiles. 'But, of course, we've only got the one girl and she's away studying at the university. Children do make such a difference in a house, don't they? Especially when there are so many of them. I thought you'd only got four.'

'I'm looking after the others while their mothers are out,' said Mrs Carruthers defiantly.

'Oh?' Mrs Withycombe gave a quasi-surprised laugh. 'I didn't realize we'd got a day nursery in the Close.'

'You haven't!' snarled Mrs Carruthers. 'I do it occasionally, just to oblige, so there's no call for you to go poking your nose in where it's not wanted.'

'The Council's very strict about licensing day nurseries,' said Mrs Withycombe, still confiding her observations to Dover.

'And quite right, too, in my opinion. Otherwise you'd have the most dreadful places springing up and ruining the tone of the neighbourhood, wouldn't you?'

Mrs Carruthers took a deep breath but Dover had had enough. 'Get on with it, MacGregor!' he snarled. 'We shall be here till midnight if you don't get a move on.'

MacGregor opened his notebook and assumed a stern and competent air. 'What, precisely, was it, madam, that you wanted to tell us?'

'Withycombe with a y,' she pointed out, watching the movement of MacGregor's pencil with great satisfaction. She was a woman who liked to be taken seriously. '14 Birdsfoot-Trefoil Close – that's the house with the new curtains and the yellow front door just opposite from poor Mrs Perking's and one down. You can't miss it. We've got leaded lights on all the front windows.' She waited until MacGregor's pencil came to a halt. 'Profession – housewife. And my husband is George Albert Withycombe and he's a foreman finisher at Wibbley's.'

'And how old are you?' asked Dover, who could see that Mrs Withycombe needed cutting down to size.

Young Mrs Carruthers chuckled in a vulgar manner and passed Dover the packet of rusks.

'Oh, I don't think we need bother about that,' said Mac-Gregor quickly after a hurried look at Mrs Withycombe's face. 'Now, can we take it that you saw or heard something which may be relevant to our inquiries?'

'Saw,' confirmed Mrs Withycombe with a sharp jerk of her head. 'Yesterday afternoon I just happened to be cleaning my front-room windows – the insides, of course. We have a man comes to do them outside.'

'And you saw something at Mrs Perking's house?' prompted MacGregor patiently.

'Yes,' said Mrs Withycombe resolutely, 'I did.'

'What was it?'

'A man.'

'Ooh!' gurgled Mrs Carruthers, giving Dover a saucy wink. 'It's getting sexy!'

'Perhaps', MacGregor suggested with a slight diminution of kindly tolerance, 'you would be good enough to give us some details. What time about was this?'

'Well, that I don't know exactly, not to the minute, that is. It was getting on for five, I should think, when I saw him walking along the road. I was thinking that before long I should have to be going to get Mr Withycombe's tea – dinner, I should say – ready, so it must have been getting on for five.'

'So you saw this man walking along the road?'

'Yes, that's right. He'd parked his car right down at the far end of the road and he came walking along on the opposite side. He came along past me and I noticed he was looking at the numbers. So, naturally, I thought he didn't quite have his bearings and so he'd left his car while he looked for the house he wanted on foot. Well, as I was saying, he passed our house on the other side of the road and then I saw him stop at Mrs Perking's house. I wasn't taking all that much notice, of course, it being no concern of mine, but I do happen to know they never have any callers. Leastways, not at the front door. So I was quite surprised to see this man open the garden gate and walk up to the front door. He rang the bell and after a bit Mrs Perking came. I could see her quite clearly and I know her very well by sight so there aren't any doubts on that score. Well, she said a few words to him and he went inside the house and they closed the door behind them.

'Well, you could have knocked me down with a feather, because, like I said, they never have any visitors, not neighbours or anybody. They keep themselves very much to themselves, the Perkings do. Of course, I've no doubt she thought herself a cut above the rest of us and with him working at that travel agency place he doesn't meet people at work like the Wibbley's men do. Still, it was none of my business. Well, naturally, I waited to see what was going to happen next. And do you know how long I had to wait? Five-and-twenty minutes if it was a second. I thought he was never coming out. I was beginning to get worried about Mr Withycombe's tea but I said to myself it wouldn't do him any harm to have to wait for once. Well, it was just beginning to get dark when I saw the front door open and out he came.'

'Did Mrs Perking let him out?' asked MacGregor.

'Not as far as I could see,' said Mrs Withycombe, relishing the attention her recital was getting, 'and I thought it was funny, even at the time. He just came out and pulled the door shut behind him. Well, I thought to myself — there's manners for you! I was always taught it was a matter of common politeness to see your visitors off the premises, but then I suppose I'm a little old-fashioned about some things. Still, I was surprised about Mrs Perking. Some people' — Mrs Withycombe just happened to be looking straight at Mrs Carruthers — 'some people you could understand but not Mrs Perking, not with her breeding.'

'What did this man do then?'

'You might well ask!' Mrs Withycombe lowered her voice dramatically. 'He pulled his hat down over his eyes, turned up his overcoat collar and all but ran back to his car as if all the devils in hell were after him! Most suspicious behaviour, if you ask me. Then he turned his car round in the road and off he shot, back the way he'd come from.'

'That would be back towards the centre of the town, would it?' asked MacGregor.

'That's right,' agreed Mrs Withycombe. 'And it was all so quick. He ran away from that house as though Satan himself was on his heels. Of course, when I got to know later on what had happened, I began to put two and two together. I said to Mr Withycombe, Albert, I said, I believe I saw Mrs Perking's murderer! And he said, well, my dear, in that case you had better go and make a statement to the police. You're right, Albert, I said, that's just what … '

'Here, hold your horses a minute!' Everybody turned to look at Dover who, up till now, had been displaying an elaborate lack of interest in what Mrs Withycombe had to say. 'When this chap left the house, was it raining?'

'Oh yes,' said Mrs Withycombe, 'pouring down it was. I remember thinking it would, just when Mr Withycombe

57

would be coming home and I'd have all his wet things cluttering up my clean kitchen.'

'Well, there you are!' snorted Dover, addressing MacGregor. 'That explains it, doesn't it? Fellow turns his collar up and hurries off to his car because he doesn't want to get wet. Nothing sinister in that, is there?'

'Well, not by itself, sir,' admitted MacGregor. 'But the timing, sir, that strikes me as being very significant.'

'It would!' Dover sniffed disparagingly and turned to Mrs Withycombe. 'Did you know this man?'

'No, I didn't.'

'Likely to recognize him again if you saw him?'

'Well,' — Mrs Withycombe was doubtful — 'I wouldn't say yes and I woudn't say no. I might, but I didn't really get a good look at his face.'

'Take a note of the car number, by any chance?'

Mrs Withycombe shook her head sadly.

'Well, that's that, isn't it?' said Dover, not unpleased by these negative answers. 'Well, thank you very much. We know where to get in touch with you if we need you.'

'Is that all?' Mrs Withycombe's face fell. She'd been preparing herself all morning for this dramatic encounter — her best coat, clean underwear and everything — and she felt she was entitled to something more than this rather off-hand dismissal.

'That's all!' said Dover flatly.

'If you don't mind, sir, I've got a few further questions that I should like to put to Mrs Withycombe.' From MacGregor's point of view it was now or never. If he didn't take the control of the investigation into his own hands at this stage, they'd finish up with yet another of Dover's typical cases in which either nobody or the wrong man was charged. MacGregor had had too much experience of the Chief Inspector's methods to harbour any doubt as to which way this one would go if the old fool were left to his own devices. He'd already got it firmly fixed in his head that John Perking had murdered his wife, and it would take much more than mere evidence to get

58

him to change his mind. In Dover's book wives were always done to death by their husbands and, if they weren't, it was up to the husbands to prove it. Since most of the bereaved husbands were unaware of the need to establish their innocence beyond a shadow of doubt, and were often in any case incapable of doing it to Dover's satisfaction, Sergeant MacGregor felt obliged to undertake their defence. He shouldered this burden in the name of justice, to uphold the dignity of the police, and to protect, as far as he could, the interests of his own career. Too many reprimands from the Director of Public Prosecutions, too many charges of false arrest, did a rising young detective no good at all.

Once he'd made up his mind to it MacGregor, in his own suave way, could be just as pig-headed as Dover. The Chief Inspector was determined to get John Perking for the murder of his wife. All right. Well, MacGregor was going to be even more determined to pin it on somebody – anybody – else. And this unknown and suspicious visitor as unmasked by the public-spirited Mrs Withycombe would do nicely for a start.

Dover appeared to have switched himself off again so Mac-Gregor jumped in with his questions while he had the chance. He smiled encouragingly at Mrs Withycombe and turned over to a clean page in his notebook.

'Do you think you could give me a full description of this man, madam? How he was dressed and everything?'

'Oh, yes!' cooed Mrs Withycombe, preening herself in the warmth of the handsome sergeant's glances.

Her optimism was unfounded. For such a talented observer of the social scene in Birdsfoot-Trefoil Close, her descriptions lacked much in the way of detail. Under MacGregor's anxious probings, however, a blurred picture eventually emerged.

The man was tall rather than short. Thin rather than fat. Young rather than old. Upright rather than stooping. His general appearance was smart rather than shabby. 'Sort of ordinary-looking altogether,' admitted Mrs Withycombe feebly.

And how was he dressed?

Mrs Withycombe plunged gallantly on to what she thought was firmer ground. Hat, raincoat, trousers and shoes. Oh, and she could almost swear that he was wearing gloves, too. Colour? Well, the raincoat was sort of lightish and the trousers were sort of darkish. The hat was a trilby and that was sort of darkish, too. Not black, she didn't think, but darkish, definitely.

'What about the car?' asked MacGregor who was beginning to get a bit snappy.

Mrs Withycombe gave a deprecating little laugh. The sergeant mustn't expect too much, she chided him playfully. Mrs Withycombe was only just an ordinary housewife, really, and not the weeniest bit mechanically minded. Cars were just cars to her. What make was it? She was sorry but she hadn't the least idea. Wasn't she an old silly?

Dover opened his eyes to see if MacGregor was going to have the guts to answer this rhetorical question.

MacGregor wasn't. 'What size was it, Mrs Withycombe?'

Oh, just an ordinary sort of size, she thought. Colour? Well, she hadn't really noticed and it was raining and she didn't really remember it being any definite sort of colour. 'It certainly wasn't bright yellow or a shocking pink,' she stated helpfully. No, she didn't know how many doors it had and it was no good asking her about the styling of the radiator because, to be perfectly honest, she wasn't sure what the radiator was anyhow. No, it definitely hadn't got a canvas roof. On that she would take her dying oath.

MacGregor, poker-faced, closed his notebook and thanked Mrs Withycombe for her co-operation. No, really, she'd been most helpful and he quite understood that if she'd known poor Mrs Perking was going to get beaten to death she would have paid more attention.

Dover yawned and rubbed one hand over his heavy jowl. 'I need a shave,' he announced. Pushing aside a wandering infant he stood up with a grunt. 'We'll go to the hotel. MacGregor, fetch the Rolls!'

Chapter Five

DOVER guzzled his way through lunch in silence. Although food was one of his few remaining pleasures, he wasn't giving all his attention to the dishes that were placed before him. He'd got other things on his mind.

Judged in retrospect, the cushy job that Mr Wibbley had all but dangled before his very eyes didn't look as enticing as it had done in the rosy light of dawn. Jammy, yes—but not really the sort of thing it was worth busting a gut over. The case was as good as solved. What difference would a few hours here or there make? Besides, it didn't do to make things look too easy. People always appreciate things more if they think you've gone to a lot of trouble over them. You'd got to look as though you were earning your money, didn't you? In fact, ruminated Dover with a rare flash of honesty, it sometimes took a damned sight more trouble to look busy than it did to do the actual work. So, that was that, wasn't it? Tomorrow would be soon enough. He'd get the whole business tied up in a hangman's noose—tomorrow.

MacGregor, too, was deep in thought. If he wanted to get his oar in before the Chief Inspector blithely arrested an innocent man, he'd have to work quickly. Dover was a hard man to please, especially if you were trying to get him to go against his most dearly cherished prejudices, and even actually change his mind. The main problem was time. When was MacGregor going to be able to escape the jealous custody of his senior officer and pursue his own lines of inquiry?

MacGregor watched carefully for the moment when Dover's dentures ground to a final halt. The brute had now been fed and would be in as amenable mood as he ever achieved.

'Have you got any plans for this afternoon, sir?' asked MacGregor innocently.

Dover regarded him with well-founded suspicion. 'Why?'

'Well, I thought there were one or two routine jobs that needed doing, sir, and I thought, if you didn't want me for anything, I might just get on with them and get them cleared out of the way.'

'What sort of jobs?'

'Well, I think we should do a house-to-house inquiry in Birdsfoot-Trefoil Close, don't you, sir? And in that row of houses that faces the back of Mrs Perking's residence. I imagine it'll be a complete waste of time and the dickens of a bore into the bargain, but I fear it's got to be done, don't you, sir?'

'Hm,' said Dover, searching for the snags. 'These routine jobs are very important, you know,' he observed piously. 'I'm for ever telling you that. Just because they're boring it doesn't mean you can shirk 'em.'

'No, sir.'

'Just house-to-house inquiries round Birdsfoot-Trefoil Close, eh?'

'That sort of thing, sir.' MacGregor was anxious not to be tied down too strictly.

'Just house-to-house inquiries round Birdsfoot-Trefoil Close,' said Dover with unmistakable finality. 'And just see that's all you do do, or I'll rip your ears off.'

'Very well, sir,' said MacGregor meekly, glad to get half a loaf at least. He glanced, as if by accident, out of the window. 'Oh dear, look at that rain! It's absolutely pouring down.'

Dover looked. It merely served to strengthen his already firm resolve. 'Drop of rain never hurt anyone,' he commented sourly. 'Well, are you going to get on with it or do you propose sitting around here all day?'

'Oh no, sir. I'm off.'

There was a pause. MacGregor didn't dare ask the question to which Dover felt, somehow, obliged to give the answer.

'I shall be staying on here for a bit,' he rumbled. 'There are one or two points about this case that need – er – thinking about. There's more to detection than leg-work,' he added aggressively.

'Oh, of course, sir. And you'll be in your room if I need to get in touch with you, sir?'

Dover nodded. 'Yes, but I don't want disturbing unless it's absolutely necessary. Understand?'

'Of course, sir.' MacGregor kept a perfectly straight face. The two Scotland Yard men went their separate ways: MacGregor out into the sooty drizzle of Pott Winckle and Dover to his hotel bedroom to have one of those quiet thinks for which he was so well known.

Dover was already halfway through his dinner before MacGregor returned. The Chief Inspector was always complaining about the vagaries of his stomach and the delicacy of his digestion but he usually proved himself a stout trencherman when presented with the opportunity.

MacGregor had entered the dining-room feeling on top of the world, but the sight of his superior officer with both feet in the trough brought back that old sinking feeling. Dover was not a pretty sight. He had still not shaved and there was now thirty-six hours of stubble adorning his pasty face. His blue serge, off-the-peg suit looked as though it had been slept in, which of course it had.

Dover regarded MacGregor with a beady and suspicious eye as the elegant young man took his place at the table. 'Oh, you're here at last, are you?'

'It was quite a big job, sir,' said MacGregor meekly and gave his order to the waiter.

'And if it wasn't, you could be trusted to make it one,' observed Dover surlily, splattering the table cloth with a half-masticated mixture of potato and gravy. 'Well, get any results — or is that asking too much?'

'On the contrary, sir,' retorted MacGregor with quite a show of spirit. 'I think we're really on to something at last. A number of ladies in Birdsfoot-Trefoil Close and its neighbourhood spend all their time peeping out of their windows and I've picked up quite a lot of useful information.'

'Such as?'

'Well, sir, for one thing Cynthia Perking wasn't having an affair or anything like that with another man. Every move she made was watched – she was quite a centre of interest, as you can well appreciate, knowing who her father was – and all her neighbours agree that nobody, apart from the odd trades-men, ever called at the house. And she was never away except for the time it took her to do her shopping and things like that. So, you see, sir,' – MacGregor stepped nervously on to for-bidden ground – 'this makes it even more unlikely that her husband killed her, doesn't it? Everybody says they were a most devoted couple and we know he'd nothing to gain finan-cially by her death. And she wasn't two-timing him with some other man. So, why should he kill her?'

Dover scowled. 'How do you know he'd no hopes of financial gain? He might have had her insured for half a million quid. Probably had. And, even if she wasn't having an affair, Perk-ing might have *thought* she was and that'd come to the same thing, wouldn't it?'

MacGregor sighed. You might as well save your breath, really.

'Is that all you've found out? Not much for a whole after-noon's work, if you ask me.'

'I got a lot more information about this mysterious caller Cynthia Perking had before she was murdered, sir.'

'Mysterious? Who says he's mysterious? He doesn't strike me as being mysterious,' rumbled Dover, eyeing MacGregor's plate with interest. 'Bit off your oats, aren't you?'

'The ladies were very hospitable, sir. I've had nineteen cups of tea and, I must confess, it's rather taken the edge off my appetite.'

'Waste not, want not,' said Dover, his fork already piercing the choicest morsels on MacGregor's plate. 'Well, get on with it, man! We don't want to be sitting here all night.'

'One of the ladies was an ex-A.T.S. driver, sir, and she took a bit more interest than most of them in the car. She reckons it was an M.G. 1100, dark green and brand new, this year anyhow. Now, that's not an especially common car, sir. There can't be all that many of them in Pott Winckle.'

'If you don't feel like facing the sweet,' said Dover, 'order the plum and apple pudding and I'll have it.'

'I did a quick check with the local police, sir. Off-hand they could only think of one person in Pott Winckle who's got a car like that.'

Dover's gaze and attention were fixed on the approaching waiter. 'Oh yes?' he said vaguely as MacGregor paused with dramatic intent.

'Young Mrs Topping-Wibbley, sir.'

Dover leaned over and grabbed MacGregor's spoon and fork. 'Damn good pudding this,' he announced. 'You should have had some. And who's young Mrs Topping-Wibbley when she's at home?'

'She's the wife of Hereward Topping-Wibbley, sir. And he is the only nephew of Daniel Wibbley himself. And, more to the point, now that Cynthia Wibbley is dead, Hereward Topping-Wibbley will presumably be Daniel Wibbley's sole heir.'

Dover mopped up the remaining juice off his plate with a piece of bread roll. 'And what is this young Mrs Topping-Wibbley? A male impersonator?'

'Of course not, sir, but her husband could have been using her car for some reason, couldn't he? His own's even more conspicuous, I understand – one of these continental sports cars made in the nineteen thirties. It's perfectly feasible that he should have borrowed his wife's car and driven to Birdsfoot-Trefoil Close in it.'

'And then murdered his cousin there?' scoffed Dover. 'Pshaw!'

'But he's got motive, sir!'

'He'll need a damned sight more than that before I start taking him seriously.'

'But look at the timing, sir.' MacGregor got out his cigarette case and offered it as a minor bribe for a morsel of the Chief Inspector's attention.

But Dover was not to be bought. Rather grandly he produced one of Daniel Wibbley's cigars from his pocket and bit the end off. 'I reckon', he remarked idly as he puffed great mouthfuls of smoke all round the dining-room, 'a drop of brandy'd go down a treat with this. It'd help settle my stomach, too.'

MacGregor signalled to the waiter. 'Well, as I was saying, sir, the timing of the murder puts Hereward Topping-Wibbley right in the centre of the picture. Now, look, sir,' – MacGregor got his notebook out and flicked over the pages – 'Cynthia Perking was killed in that front room some time between four thirty and six thirty. There was a good fire and the television was on. Now, we know from Mrs Carruthers that Cynthia always watched this serial *For Better or Worse* every afternoon. She *never* missed. The serial ends at five forty-five p.m. and, as soon as it finished, she switched off and went into the kitchen to start getting the supper ready. So, since she was killed in the front room, she must have been killed *before* five forty-five, mustn't she? Otherwise she wouldn't have been in the front room at all, she'd have been in the kitchen. Now, on the night of the murder, John Perking didn't return home until ten past six – but his wife was already dead by then. She must have been. So we've got to start looking for somebody who was in that house before a quarter to six, and we've found him.

'Now, we've no proof yet, sir, that this man who called on Cynthia Perking was in fact Hereward Topping-Wibbley, but I'm pretty confident that he's our man. Just look how he behaved, sir! He uses a borrowed car, because anybody in the town would spot his a mile off, he parks it some distance away from the house and walks – in the rain – the rest of the way. Why – unless he doesn't want to be noticed? Cynthia Perking lets him into the house about five o'clock. Naturally she takes him into the front room. Now, the next bit's speculation, sir, but this is my guess as to what happened. He has a quarrel with Cynthia, sees the poker there, picks it up and kills her. Or, better still, she tells him that at long last she's going to have a baby. You can see what that was going to mean to him, can't you, sir? It puts paid to his hopes of eventually taking over

66

control of the Wibbley organization. But with Cynthia *and* **her** child out of the way, he's sitting pretty. He'll get the lot.

'All the details fit, too, sir. There are no fingerprints in that room that they can't identify – apart from a couple of sets that I think are yours, sir. All the rest belong to Cynthia Perking or her husband. But, we *know* Hereward Topping-Wibbley **was** wearing gloves. Mrs Withycombe said so. So that's what I think happened sir. Topping-Wibbley grabs the poker, **kills** Cynthia, lets himself quietly out of the house, gets in his **car** and drives off. He thinks no one's seen him or, at any **rate,** recognized him. According to Mrs Withycombe – and **her** evidence is supported by others – he was in that house for about half an hour and nobody saw Cynthia Perking alive after he left it. It's cast iron, sir.'

'So are sieves!' snorted Dover. He ground out his cigar **in** his coffee cup. 'Here, give me one of your fags to take the **taste** away. I reckon that cigar's gone off a bit.'

'But you do admit there's a pretty solid case against Topping-Wibbley, don't you, sir?'

Dover pursed his lips judicially. 'No,' he said, after **giving** the matter a moment's cursory thought, 'I don't. If you **ask** me it's a load of old cod's wallop. You want to watch **that** imagination of yours, laddie. It'll be getting you into **serious** trouble one of these days.'

'Well, if you can see any flaws in my theory,' said Mac-Gregor huffily, 'I should be grateful if you'd point them out to me, sir.'

'Trouble is', said Dover, undoing the top button of **his** trousers, 'to know where to start. That's better! I hope **my** stomach's not going to start playing me up again. I've been **a** bit constipated the last few days and that's always a bad **sign.** Remind me to take a dose of salts tonight, laddie. Now then – flaws! Right! Well, was this murder premeditated or unpre-meditated?'

'Er – premeditated, sir, definitely. Why park his car so **far** away from the house? Why borrow a car in the first place?'

'But, if it was premeditated, you nit, bang goes his motive!

You say he killed Cynthia Perking because she was pregnant. Well, how did he know? She'd only found out for sure herself that morning.'

'Well ... ' began MacGregor.

'You can't have it both ways, laddie. And if it wasn't premeditated, bang goes all this business about him using somebody else's car and parking it away from the house. Castles in the air, laddie, that's what you're building! You've been reading too many of these daft detective stories. Take it from me, laddie, real-life crime's not like that.' Dover belched comfortably.

MacGregor tried again. 'I think ... '

'Look, laddie,' growled Dover, his temporary good humour deserting him rapidly, 'we're not going to spend all night flogging a dead horse. Hereward Topping-Wibbley is a non-starter! Get it? Cynthia Perking was done in by her husband and tomorrow morning you can push off bright and early and get a warrant for him. Then we'll nip over to his sister's place and arrest the bastard. This is an open-and-shut case and I'm damned if I'm having you making a four-course meal out of it. And you'd better look up the trains back to London after lunch too, while you're about it.'

MacGregor was appalled. For a few seconds he couldn't think of anything to say and watched in stunned silence as Dover helped himself to another cigarette. If somebody didn't do something, the old fool would just steamroller his way to black disaster. Mentally awarding himself the Victoria Cross MacGregor took his courage in both hands. 'Sir, I really must protest. No, please, sir – let me have my say. If you don't, I shall really feel obliged to put in an official complaint.'

'You cheeky young bugger!' gasped Dover. 'After all I've done for you! Talk about biting the hand that feeds you, this takes the bleeding biscuit!'

'I'm sorry, sir, but I mean it,' said MacGregor stoutly. 'You simply can't just waltz off and arrest John Perking like that – simply because you've got a general theory about wife murderers. Good heavens, sir, you haven't even clapped eyes on

John Perking yet, never mind questioned him. He may be able to clear himself quite easily, apart from the fact that in my considered opinion his wife was already dead long before he got back home from work.'

'All right,' roared Dover, his little black moustache twitching with fury, 'I'll just damned well prove to you here and now that Perking killed her! I was trying to spare your feelings but I can see now that such consideration on my part is like water off a dead duck's back. Now, just pin those shell-like lug-holes of yours well back, sergeant, and listen! Call yourself a detective? You've about as much blasted idea of detecting as … ' Once again Dover couldn't think of a suitable simile so he abandoned the search. 'Yesterday afternoon, from the time Cynthia Perking left her next-door neighbour's until the time that copper off the cars confirmed that she was dead, only two people entered that house. Agreed? One was your mysterious stranger who may or may not be Hereward Topping-Wibbley and the other was the dead woman's husband. Right?'

'As far as we know, sir.'

'As far as we know at the moment, but if you think a mouse could have got in without one of those nosey women spotting it you've got more faith in human nature than I have. Now, your chap calls and goes away again. I don't know why he called and you don't know why he called. It doesn't bloody well matter. When he left Cynthia Perking was still alive.'

'Mrs Withycombe didn't see her, sir,' MacGregor pointed out sulkily. 'She said … '

'Yacking again, MacGregor? You can't stop that mouth of yours flapping for two minutes, can you? It's a pity you don't talk less and use what passes for your brains a bit more. What about the bloody television set?'

'The television set, sir?'

'Yes,' lisped Dover in a crude attempt at mimicking his sergeant's more cultured tones, 'the television set, sir! Look in your little notebook and see what the policeman who examined the body had to say about the television set.'

'I can remember perfectly well, as it happens, sir. He said

that when he entered the room where Mrs Perking was lying the television set – which she had been watching – was still on. He even remembered what the programme was and, when he checked, he found that the set was still switched on to the station Mrs Perking used to watch every afternoon.'

'Well,' said Dover, assuming a heavy condescending manner which made MacGregor long to kick him where it would do most good, 'of course I don't know how they do things in the elevated social circles in which you move, but in my humble environment we switch the telly *off* when guests arrive. Matter of common politeness, I should have thought. Now, just work it out for yourself, laddie. Cynthia Perking is sitting there watching the telly. At five o'clock the front-door bell rings. She goes to answer it and brings the caller back into the sitting-room. She switches off the telly and they have their little chat or what-have-you. His lordship or whoever-it-is stays until twenty-five past five. "Don't bother coming to the front door," he says all polite-like, "I'll see myself out." "O.K.," she says with one eye on the clock, and out he goes. She makes a dive for the television set and switches it on. She's in time to see the last ten minutes or so of her precious serial. You know what these telly addicts are like: half a programme's better than nothing. And that, my clever young gentleman, is why the telly was on. If your mysterious visitor had done her in that television set would have been off, wouldn't it?'

To say that MacGregor was staggered would be an under-statement. Of course the blundering old goon was barking up the wrong tree, but he'd produced quite a logical little piece of deduction. In all their long and unhappy association MacGregor had never heard him achieve anything like it before. It was rather touching, really. To have thought it all out so carefully and to be so utterly wrong.

MacGregor gave his boss an encouraging smile. He'd have to handle this tactfully. 'Hereward Topping-Wibbley might have switched the television set on after killing Mrs Perking and before he left the house, mightn't he, sir?'

'What the hell for?' demanded Dover pugnaciously.

'Well, to put us off the scent, sir,' MacGregor suggested with a playful little laugh.

Dover blurted out a very rude word. It exploded into the comparative quiet of the dining-room and an elderly clergyman at the far end nearly spilt his Bloody Mary.

'I say, steady on, sir!'

'Much more of your damned patronizing, MacGregor, and I'll swing for you, so help me I will! I'm blowed if I know what you think you've got to be so blasted smug about. I've been trying to let you down gently because I didn't want to discourage you but I can see I've been wasting my breath. If you used your eyes half as much as you use your mouth you'd have seen it for yourself.'

MacGregor frowned. 'Seen what, sir?'

'The kitchen, you stupid young whelp! If you're a sample of the rising generation of coppers, the villains are in for a right old field-day. Look – the unknown caller leaves the Perking's house at twenty-five past five or so. Cynthia Perking watches the tail end of her television serial. The she turns the set off and ... '

'But you just said ... '

'If you don't hold your tongue!' gobbled Dover in an excess of fury. 'She turned the bloody set off, went into the kitchen and started getting the bloody supper ready. At ten past six, or whatever blasted time it was, John Perking comes home on his bloody bicycle. On some pretext or another he lures his wife back into the front room. There he picks up the bloody poker and bashes her brains out. Then he builds the fire up because he knows a high temperature is going to make fixing the time of death more difficult, *and* he switches on the telly. Then he rushes back into the kitchen and removes all traces of the fact that his wife was getting the supper ready. He tries to make it look as though she'd never started – and, as far as morons like you are concerned, he succeeded. Then he heads for the front door, pausing only to rip the telephone wires out in the hall. That's to give him a bit more time, see? It all helps to confuse things. Now, what time was it when he phoned the police?'

71

'Er —'—MacGregor searched hurriedly through his note-book—'six twenty-nine, sir.'

'Twenty bloody minutes!' snorted Dover. 'He'd all the time in the world.'

MacGregor stared thoughtfully at his notebook. He didn't like the way things were developing at all. Suppose that, just for once, by some miracle, Dover had got it right?

'You didn't bother to have a proper look round that kitchen, did you, laddie?'

'The fingerprint boys still hadn't quite finished when I went back there after lunch today, sir, and … '

'But I looked,' said Dover, waggling a fat and reproving finger, 'before the fingerprint boys even got there. You remember me looking, don't you, laddie? You thought I was bugger-ing all the clues up, didn't you? You didn't realize that I was just solving the whole perishing case while you floundered around doing things by the book. Do you know what Mr and Mrs Perking were going to have for their supper that night, laddie?'

Dumbly MacGregor shook his head.

'They were going to have chop and chips and fried tomatoes and if, when you've got a moment to spare, you care to look in that little plastic dustbin thing, you'll find the whole bang-shoot in there. Now, I know Cynthia Perking wasn't supposed to be any great shakes as a housekeeper but I don't think she was so feckless as to chuck two perfectly good, partly cooked chops, a pile of raw chips and four tomatoes away just for the hell of it, do you? Why the blazes should she? And I'll tell you something else, laddie, since, being a bachelor, you haven't been house-trained yet. Women are creatures of habit. Cynthia Perking was quite a tidy-minded person really—you can see that from the house. So when I find just two knives and two forks and a couple of pudding spoons chucked all higgledy-piggledy in the cutlery drawer I start thinking that, maybe, she didn't put them away. Dover looked contemptu-ously at MacGregor. 'I could tell you practically every move Perking made in that kitchen—tablecloth not folded in the folds, basket in the chip pan all twisted round the wrong way—but I can't be bothered. Tomorrow morning, after we've arrested Mr John Perking, you can go round there and work it out for yourself.'

MacGregor opened his mouth but, not being able to think of anything appropriate to say, helplessly shut it again.

Chapter Six

THE following morning Dover was, not surprisingly, most intolerably cock-a-hoop. It wasn't often that he could chalk up such a triumph and he had no intention of letting his moment of glory run to waste. With undisguised glee he set about rubbing MacGregor's nose in it as hard as he could. That young gentleman, considerably shaken, had to suffer in silence as his Chief Inspector swaggered around the hotel, bawling his head off and telling indignant chambermaids to jump to it and show a leg there.

It was nearly ten o'clock before MacGregor got back, armed with a warrant for the arrest of John Perking and accompanied by a local C.I.D. inspector to serve it. The comparative lateness of the hour was not entirely due to the time wasted by Dover's display of histrionics. MacGregor, a bit of a Doubting Thomas where his Chief Inspector was concerned, hadn't been able to resist making a quick visit to Birdsfoot-Trefoil Close, just to check. The technical experts from the Regional Crime Squad were still there, stretching out a cushy job as long as they could. They knew all about the good food thrown to waste in the yellow plastic pedal bin. They had spotted the disorder in the cutlery drawer and the inaccurately folded tablecloth. And they had drawn the correct conclusions. They watched MacGregor in some surprise as he swiftly went over ground which they, humble provincials with straw in their hair, had long since covered.

'Keep your shirt on, sarge,' advised one greying photographer who, even in Pott Winckle, had seen it all. 'We haven't missed anything. You'll have my artistic pictures by lunchtime. When are you making the arrest?'

'Er – this morning, I think,' MacGregor answered, praying

quite hard that a merciful Providence would vouchsafe him some irrefutable evidence with which to scotch Dover's theory.

'And that'll be curtains for John Perking, eh? He won't have a leg to stand on when the jury get an eyeful of all this.' He waved an indifferent hand round the kitchen. 'Bit of luck for you lot, isn't it?'

'Isn't what?'

'Well, rushing down here all the way from London to solve a crime a kid of seven wouldn't have lost any sleep over. Blowed if I can think why you didn't make an arrest last night.'

'Things are not always as simple as they seem,' said Mac-Gregor severely, and hoped he was right.

Back at the hotel Dover was storming around in the entrance hall like a dyspeptic admiral on his quarter deck. 'And about time, too!' he bellowed as MacGregor shepherded the local inspector through the swing doors.

'This is Inspector Mansion, sir, of the Regional Crime Squad.'

Dover eyed the newcomer up and down with his habitual sneer. 'Got the warrant? Right, well, Mansion, or whatever your name is, I want this arrest made quickly and efficiently. Get it? I'm not the man to tolerate anything slip-shod. Clear?'

'I have made arrests before, sir.'

'Ah, but not for me though, have you?' retorted Dover with the air of one revealing the hidden truths of nature.

'No, sir.' Inspector Mansion's face was quite blank and his voice expressionless. 'I haven't yet had that pleasure.'

Dover glared suspiciously at him. Was that dumb insolence or not? He couldn't quite decide and vented his frustration on MacGregor by sending him upstairs to fetch his hat and coat.

They made quite an impressive little convoy as they turned into Canal Bank Street. Two motor-cycle policemen rode ahead, steely-eyed behind their goggles. Next came a black police car with MacGregor and Inspector Mansion sitting in an embarrassed silence in the back. As in royal processions the cynosure of all eyes came at the end: Detective Chief Inspector Dover, lolling amongst the cushions of his borrowed Rolls-Royce smoking a big cigar and coughing.

The kids in Canal Bank Street stopped playing 'Bashing Perking's Bint' and stared with shrewd calculating little eyes.

'Come on!' shouted one golden-haired tot. 'It's the bleeding rozzers!' Her playmates tore after her down the street in the hopeful but mistaken impression that they were going to witness a topping on their very doorstep.

Their mums were more worldly-wise, but just as interested. They appeared as if by magic on the thresholds of their terraced houses and, in flowered overalls and curlers, nodded their satisfaction to each other.

'Told you they'd be coming for him before long,' they said to their next-door neighbours and complacently folded their arms, happy to see one husband about to receive his just deserts.

The door of Number 25 opened. A young woman stood there, correctly dressed in the uniform of the street. She had a bright, intelligent face but she looked strained. Automatically she, too, folded her arms.

'Yes?' she asked defiantly as if she had no idea what the three large men had come for. She refused to look at the group of uniformed policemen who were standing dourly on the edge of the scene, waiting to play their parts.

'We're police officers,' said Inspector Mansion.

'Oh, really? Well, what can I do for you?'

'We'd like to have a word with your brother, miss. Is he in?'

'I'll just go and see,' she replied, playing the farce through to the end. 'Hang on a minute.'

But, as she turned away from the door, Inspector Mansion followed by Dover and MacGregor crowded into the minute hall behind her. The uniformed policemen moved closer.

The back kitchen wasn't much bigger than the hall. John Perking was sitting at the table, a large white mug of tea and a newspaper in front of him. He was in his shirtsleeves. No collar. His attitude was patently antagonistic but his face showed no emotion when he looked up.

Inspector Mansion was equally intent on avoiding dramatics. 'John Alexander Perking?' he asked. 'I have a warrant here for your arrest on a charge of murdering your wife, Cynthia Rosalind Perking. I must warn you that you are not obliged to say anything or make any statement unless you wish to do so, but anything you do say will be taken down in writing and may be used in evidence.'

John Perking stared bleakly at the inspector. 'She was dead when I got home,' he muttered at last and watched his words being duly written down.

'What happens now?' asked Perking's sister. 'We've always been a respectable family, we have. You'll have to tell us what he's got to do.'

'I shall want him to accompany me to the police station, miss,' said Inspector Mansion imperturbably. 'Where's your coat, Perking?'

'It's upstairs,' snapped the sister irritably, 'and so's his shoes. You don't want to take him in his slippers, do you? And don't keep calling me miss. I've been married these seven years and my name's Mrs Stafford.'

'I beg your pardon, madam. Well, one of my constables will accompany him upstairs to get his things and then we'll be off.' He nodded to Perking who got to his feet and began to slouch out of the room.

'Can he have a shave before he goes?' asked Mrs Stafford.

'I don't think we want to waste too much time, madam. He can have a shave at the station if he wants one. Taylor,' he shouted out into the hall, 'you go up with him! And just get a move on!'

There was a considerable amount of shuffling and pushing as Perking and Inspector Mansion got themselves out of the kitchen, leaving Dover and MacGregor behind. Glumly Dover sat himself down in a comfortable armchair by the fire while the sergeant, not quite knowing what to do, hovered uncertainly by the door.

Footsteps could be heard mounting the stairs and then thudding about in the room above the kitchen. Confused mumbles came from the men waiting in the hall. Footsteps coming down the stairs. More confused sound of low voices. The front door opened. The front door closed.

Mrs Stafford sat down abruptly in the chair her brother had just vacated.

'Well, don't say I didn't warn him!' she said with a viciousness that made even Dover blink. 'I knew no good would ever come of it, I knew that right from the start. You'll live to regret it, I told him, mark my words you'll live to regret it. And,' she added with a sour laugh, 'he has. Perhaps he'll listen to me next time.' She looked across at MacGregor. 'What happens now?'

'They'll bring him up before the magistrates in the morning and I imagine they'll remand him for trial at the next assizes.'

She sighed. 'Magistrates! Trial! Assizes! Thank God our mum isn't alive to see it. It'd kill her. She'd die of the shame. What do we do about getting him a lawyer to defend him?'

'Well, I imagine the magistrates'll grant him legal aid and they'll tell him what to do down at the station. You haven't got a solicitor, I suppose.'

She shook her head.

'Well, if he's got the money, of course, he can … '

'Money? He hasn't got two ha'pennies to rub together. That wasn't a bad job, you know, at that travel agency and he got quite good money, considering. If he'd stayed on round here he'd have been in clover. If she's going to marry you, I told him, she ought to put up with what you've had to put up with all your life. Course that was the end of it, me saying that I mean. It's been his one ambition ever since he was a kid – to get out of Canal Bank Street.' She sighed again. 'Has either of you two fellows got a fag? He smoked my last and I don't fancy going out to the corner shop this morning. Well, Canal Bank Street's had the last laugh, hasn't it? We've never been mixed up in a murder before. Ta, love!' She took one of

MacGregor's cigarettes and drew the smoke deep down into her lungs. 'Ever since he was a tiny kid! They're not going to carry my coffin down Canal Bank Street, he used to say. He hated it here. He thought when he got into the grammar school that he was on his way, but he wasn't good enough. Not to go to a university or anything. Some lads at sixteen would have cleared out and gone off on their own, but our kid didn't have enough guts for that. He wouldn't go into Wibbley's, though. That he had made his mind up about. In the end he got this job in this travel agency. Told us that it was a real step up in the world. Our dad just couldn't fathom it. It's longer hours for less pay, he used to tell him, and you've no union at the back of you. He was all for the union, our dad was.' Her eyes filled with tears. 'He died last year, you know. Only a few months after my mum. Neither of 'em was fifty. You just can't understand it, can you? They'd been decent hard-working people all their lives and then they just go and die like that. Still,' – she choked back a sob – 'I suppose it was all for the best, seeing what's happened now.'

MacGregor made sympathetic noises but Dover evinced a more practical turn of mind. 'Why don't you make yourself a nice cup of tea,' he suggested. 'Do you good, a nice cup of tea would. I wouldn't say no to one myself.'

'I'll bet you wouldn't,' retorted Mrs Stafford tartly and blew her nose. 'Priests and coppers, our dad used to say, they'd share your last crust with you.' She got up and filled the kettle at the sink.

But Dover didn't want to stop her talking. 'You reckon your brother made a mistake in marrying Cynthia Wibbley, do you?'

'Well, what do you think? He'd hardly be accused of murdering her if he'd never met her, would he?'

'How did he meet her exactly?'

'Well, he joined this tennis club. Laugh? Our dad near ruptured himself when he heard. That was before he found out there was three guineas' subscription to pay every year, of course.'

'And Cynthia Wibbley was a member, too?'

'Good grief, no! You just don't understand, do you? The Wibbleys are like royalty round here. Cynthia might have gone along to present the prizes and graciously accept a bouquet but she wouldn't ever play there. No, it was this other girl, Mildred Denny — she was the one our Jack was after. She's some sort of poor relation of the Wibbleys but, of course, she was a cut above the rest of the tennis club and our Jack was really taken with her. I don't think he'd ever thought of marrying his way out of Canal Bank Street before but when he found she'd taken a fancy to him he began to get some really big ideas. I told him he wanted his head examining but you might as well have talked to a brick wall.' She got the best cups and saucers out of a cupboard and put them on the table. 'I mean, how old was he then? Twenty? And she was twenty-seven if she was a day and no oil painting. Why's nobody wanted to marry her before, I asked him. Because she's as poor as a church mouse and because she looks like something the cat brought in, that's why. He wouldn't listen, of course. Took it for granted that because she lived in a big house and called Mr Wibbley "Uncle Daniel" she must be rolling in it.' She warmed the teapot and reached for the caddy. 'Mind you, I blame her as much as our Jack. Talk about cradle snatching! And the gossip! Our dad used to dread having to go to work of a morning. The whole town knew about it and they were laughing themselves fit to bust. One of the Wibbleys' lot carrying on with a kid of a clerk from Canal Bank Street! Not that she was a proper Wibbley — only by marriage, of course. Do you both take milk and sugar? Well, she was the one who introduced our Jack to Cynthia. Took him along to a tennis party at the big house and that was where she made her big mistake. Because Cynthia was only eighteen, she wasn't bad-looking and her dad was a millionaire. Our Jack fell in love with *her* on the spot. It was just like something out of a blooming film.'

'Was he really in love with her?'

Mrs Stafford shrugged her shoulders. 'You tell me. He

might have married her if she hadn't had a farthing to her name, I suppose, but he never really had to face up to that sort of a decision, did he?'

'I thought Mr Wibbley slung her out without a penny?'

'Oh, our Jack didn't take that seriously. He thought the old bastard'd come round, given time. Cynthia was his only child, after all, and there was never really any question but that she would come in to it all when her dad dies. Mind you, I reckon our Jack thought that if Cynthia'd bend a bit and suck up to the old fellow everything'd be forgotten and forgiven. But she was as stiff-necked as old Wibbley, from what I gather. She wouldn't go cap in hand to him and our Jack couldn't make her. This last few months or so, though, I thought he'd got reconciled to just having to sweat it out.'

'Suppose there had been children?' asked Dover slyly.

'Ah, well – that would have made a difference, wouldn't it? That'd have brought the old man round quicker than anything. They badly wanted a kid but, as my husband says, you've got to do more than want. Another cup?'

'Did you know your sister-in-law was pregnant?'

'What?' The teapot dropped with a crash on to the table. Mrs Stafford gaped at Dover. 'Never!'

'She was, you know.'

'Well, I don't know what to say. Our Jack can't have known it, that's for sure.'

'We're pretty certain he did.'

'Well,' said Mrs Stafford, shaking her head so that the curlers rattled, 'I'll go to our house! That takes the biscuit, that does! I mean, I couldn't understand what had got into him before, but if she was expecting … ' She shook her head again. 'Well, he must have had a brainstorm or something, that's all I can think of.'

'Like hell he did!' snarled Dover who wasn't having any of that defeatist talk. 'He did it in cold blood – and he tried to cover up his traces afterwards. It wasn't a bad effort but, of course, it didn't fool me for a minute.'

MacGregor decided to cut short what might possibly develop

into a trumpet voluntary. 'You appear to think that your brother is guilty, Mrs Stafford,' he said gently.

She looked doubtfully at him and then shrugged her shoulders with weary resignation. 'I can always tell. I could ever since he was a little nipper. He used to think he was being as clever as a box of monkeys but he couldn't pull the wool over my eyes. Not that I claim to understand it, mind. I couldn't before and now you say she was expecting ... Well, it's beyond me. I mean, why should he? He thought the world of her, you know, really. I mean, there she was – the great Daniel Wibbley's daughter – and out of all the men in the world she'd chosen him. And it hadn't been made easy for her, had it? She'd defied her father, she'd sacrificed a life of luxury – and all for our Jack. Any man'd be flattered, wouldn't he? He was terribly grateful to her. She made him feel like Robert Taylor and one of the Beatles and I don't know who all rolled into one.'

'Maybe there was another woman?' asked Dover hopefully.

'Never in your life! You ask anybody. It must have been a brainstorm. What reason could he possibly have for doing a dreadful thing like that?'

Dover's bottom lip pouted out. He was beginning to go off Mrs Stafford. She made a good nourishing cup of tea but all this talk about brainstorms was getting on his wick.

'She has got a point though, hasn't she, sir?' said MacGregor when they were once more reclining in the Rolls.

'No!' snapped Dover, pulling down the folding seat opposite and putting his feet on it. 'She knows he's as guilty as hell so what else can she say? They make me sick, they do. Every-thing-suddenly-went-black-and-I-can't-remember-a-thing. It's the classic defence.'

'But there doesn't seem the faintest hint of a motive, does there, sir?'

'Look, laddie,' – Dover was getting fed up with this con-tinual carping and niggling – 'we've enough evidence on Perking to pin this job on him a dozen times over. Even you ought to be able to see that. It's all there, as clear as crystal.

We haven't had to fiddle a blind thing. He's put the noose round his own neck without any assistance from us. You want to count your blessings, you do. You don't get a case as open and shut as this once in a lifetime. We don't have to go working ourselves up into a muck sweat about motives. He's got one all right, don't you worry. There's none of this amnesia lark going to wash here. So now, let it drop, will you? I was sent down here to find Cynthia Perking's murderer and I've found him. What more do you want – blood on it?'

'But it's not me, sir,' protested MacGregor. 'It's when the case comes up in court and … '

'Oh, shut up!' snarled Dover.

MacGregor gazed miserably out of the window. 'Where are we going now, sir?'

'Going to see Mr Wibbley,' rumbled Dover sulkily.

Mr Wibbley? MacGregor repressed a sigh. What were they going to see Mr Wibbley for, of all people? Oh well, his not to reason why, his just to tag along and pick up the pieces. He slipped off into his favourite day-dream in which a beaming Assistant Commissioner at New Scotland Yard informed him that his years of suffering were over and he was being assigned to another – any other – senior detective. MacGregor was just mentally falling on his knees and seizing the Assistant Commissioner's hand prior to covering it with tear-soaked kisses of gratitude when a bulky elbow rammed in his ribs brought him back to sordid reality.

'I'm waiting', Dover informed him icily, 'for you to open the blasted door for me!'

The interview with Daniel Wibbley was not a success. Dover, fondly expecting to be hailed as the hero of the hour, made the tactical error of taking MacGregor in with him. Side by side the two of them tramped across several acres of carpet, lured by the distant prospect of Mr Wibbley's colossal desk. When they finally arrived they were not asked to sit down. Indeed, for several minutes Mr Wibbley didn't take any notice of them at all. He sat in an expensive leather-covered chair, his back to an impressive view of the Wibbley works as seen through an enormous floor-to-ceiling plate-glass window. Mr Wibbley read calmly through to the end of several typewritten sheets of foolscap and then laid them neatly on his desk.

'I see from this report on the post mortem that my daughter was two months pregnant at the time of her decease.'

'So we understand,' said Dover, moving uneasily from one throbbing foot to the other.

'Was her husband aware of this?'

'It seems likely,' said Dover.

'Mm.' Mr Wibbley swivelled round in his chair and contemplated the view. There was a long, long pause. 'What progress have you to report so far?'

'Oh, it's all over, Mr Wibbley. We've finished. John Perking was arrested on a charge of murder not half an hour ago.'

Mr Wibbley swivelled sharply back again. 'Indeed? That was quick work.'

'Well, I must admit I'm not much of a one for mucking about,' smirked Dover modestly. 'You won't catch me letting the grass ... '

'I trust that it is not also slipshod work. When this matter comes to trial it is imperative that the case for the prosecution is absolutely watertight. I want no "ifs" and "buts" about it. I want it proved beyond the slightest shadow of doubt that Perking murdered my daughter with malice aforethought, that he had a motive for murdering her – preferably some form of sordid personal gain – and that no one else could conceivably have perpetrated the crime. Perking is not a fool. With the assistance of an unscrupulous lawyer he will doubtless try to establish any number of bolt-holes. I want them all stopped up. I do not wish the judge and jury to be inveigled into giving that young whelp the benefit of any doubt whatsoever.'

'Oh, quite,' said Dover, the smirk beginning to seep off his face.

'You are quite confident that this has been achieved?'

Dover cleared his throat. 'Oh, yes.'

'And you, sergeant?'

MacGregor all but jumped out of his skin as this question was suddenly barked at him. 'Me, sir?' he stammered.

'Yes, you!'

'Well … ' MacGregor was in somewhat of a quandary. Personal integrity and loyalty to his senior officer struggled within him. Personal integrity should have won hands down but the Chief Inspector could turn very nasty at times. Especially when he was crossed. MacGregor gulped. 'It's rather difficult to give you that kind of assurance, sir,' he floundered. 'It's very rarely that we can tie up absolutely every loose end. In any investigation there are always a few points which don't seem to fit into the general pattern.' He shot a sideways glance at Dover's blood-infused and lowering face. 'Just minor points, of course, sir.'

'Let's be hearing them,' said Mr Wibbley grimly.

MacGregor looked appealingly at Dover. Dover scowled ferociously back.

'Come on!' snapped Mr Wibbley. 'If there are some discrepancies we'll have them now – not sprung on us in the assize court.'

MacGregor sighed. He had been pushed across the Rubicon. 'Well, sir, I'm not entirely happy about Perking's motive for the murder. There seems to be no material gain involved for him and they appear to have been a very devoted couple. The only cloud on their horizon appears to have been the lack of a child, and yet Perking is supposed to have killed his wife within hours of hearing that she was at last pregnant.'

Dover opened his mouth.

'You hold your tongue!' rasped Mr Wibbley. 'Anything else, sergeant?'

'Well, sir, on the afternoon that she was murdered Mrs Perking had a visitor. This in itself was most unusual becuase, according to the neighbours, nobody ever called. The visitor, a man, left at about twenty-five past five. Mrs Perking was not seen alive after he left the house and, according to the doctor's estimate, the murder could have taken place as early as half past four, sir.'

'Who is this man?'

'We don't know,' Dover broke in irritably. 'It's of no damned importance, anyhow. Perking definitely killed your daughter and I can prove that to the blasted satisfaction of any court in the world.'

'I told you at our first interview,' said Mr Wibbley, 'that I wished no stone to be left unturned. There are evidently two very large stones here which have not even been touched. It appears to me that the arrest of Perking has been somewhat premature. The lack of credible motive is especially serious. I don't want Perking pleading temporary insanity or diminished responsibility or whatever it is. There must not be the slightest shred of sympathy for him, either at the trial or in later years when his case comes up for review. Nobody is going to murder my daughter and get away with it by sitting in a warm comfortable prison for three or four years.'

'Now, look here,' Dover began to bluster, 'we've got more than enough evidence to blooming well ... '

'No, Chief Inspector!' Mr Wibbley pressed one of the buttons on his desk. 'I think I must ask you to continue your investigations. I cannot, of course,'—a mock rueful laugh—'insist. Should you run into any difficulties with your superiors at New Scotland Yard about the length of time you are staying in Pott Winckle, I suggest that you just mention my name to your Commissioner. Good morning.'

Chapter Seven

'JUDAS!' snarled Dover.

'I'm sorry, sir, but he sort of caught me off-balance,' Mac-Gregor lied uncomfortably. 'Before I really knew what was happening I'd sort of blurted it out.'

'Saboteur!' snarled Dover.

'But isn't it really better, sir, to stay on for a couple of days or so and do the job properly?'

'Sneak!' snarled Dover.

'There'd only be trouble later on at the trial, sir, if Perking's defence raised any doubts.'

'Tell-tale!' snarled Dover.

'And if Mr Wibbley really does know the Commissioner, sir ... '

'Communist!' snarled Dover.

MacGregor grabbed the menu off the table and passed it over. 'Would you like to see what you're going to have for lunch, sir?'

Dover ignored the olive branch. 'I've no appetite, thanks to you!' His stomach rumbled loudly. 'There! Did you hear that? That's what happens when I'm faced with downright disloyalty – it gets me straight in the gut!'

'A little boiled fish, sir?'

Dover snatched the menu out of MacGregor's hand and cast a practised eye over it. 'Tomato soup,' he announced, 'steak-and-kidney pie, boiled potatoes and butter beans. and roly-poly-pudding.'

'Would you like something to drink, sir?'

A suspicious gleam came into Dover's beady little eyes. 'You wouldn't be trying to soft-soap me, laddie, would you?'

'Of course not, sir.'

'All right. Well, I'll have a pint of best draught bitter.'

The hotel dining-room was once more the scene of high-powered, top-level discussions. The real points at issue were never brought out in the open. MacGregor wanted to spend the afternoon pursuing his own independent lines of inquiry and Dover wanted to retire to his room for a quiet think, secure in the knowledge that his sergeant wasn't getting up to any mischief. In the end the usual fairly satisfactory compromise was reached: Dover retired to bed and MacGregor was let loose to perform a series of routine and boring tasks which his lord and master was confident would lead nowhere.

When MacGregor called to escort Dover down to dinner he was not surprised to find him lying flat on his back on the bed, shoeless, collarless and covered with the eiderdown. He was surprised, however, to find that the old fool had not spent the entire afternoon in the arms of Morpheus.

'I've been thinking,' said Dover.

'Oh yes, sir?' MacGregor was a very well brought up young man.

'Perking,' announced Dover and belched loudly.

'Sir?'

'Well, he'll know, won't he?'

'Know, sir?'

'Why he killed his wife, you damned fool!'

'So far, sir, he's absolutely refusing to make a statement. Mr Wibbley's right. Perking is no fool. The less he says the better from his point of view.'

'Ah, Wibbley,' ruminated Dover. 'He struck me as a very decent type of chap at first but I've gone off him. Right off him.'

'He's quite shrewd, sir.'

'And so am I, laddie, so am I!' boomed Dover indignantly. 'So Perking won't talk, eh? Well, we shall have to see about that.' He rolled into a sitting position on the edge of the bed and scratched his stomach thoughtfully.

MacGregor's heart sank. 'You're not thinking of interviewing him yourself, are you, sir?'

88

Dover's fat face split into a wicked grin. 'What else? I've cracked tougher nuts than him in my time.' He stretched out one arm and clenched the podgy fist. Slabs of fat on his biceps twitched sluggishly as he flexed his muscles. 'By the look of him, our Mr Perking shouldn't give me much trouble.'

MacGregor's throat was dry. 'When were you proposing to go and see him, sir?'

'Oh, later on tonight – or, rather, early tomorrow morning. That's when their resistance is lowest, you know, in the small hours. We'll wake him up about two o'clock, say, and see if we can't persuade him to be a bit more co-operative, eh? And, if he won't listen to the voice of sweet reason, well,' – he clenched his fist again and waggled it under MacGregor's nose – 'there are other methods.'

'You can't, sir!' protested MacGregor in horror.

'Oh, can't I? It's been done before, laddie, and it'll be done again. There's no danger if there aren't any witnesses – then it's just your word against his, see? And who's going to believe a lousy wife murderer?'

'But, sir, he's up before the magistrates first thing in the morning. If he shows signs of having been beaten up, there'll be the very devil of a row.'

'Don't they teach you anything on these courses you're for ever skiving off on?' said Dover disgustedly. In the first place you take damned good care not to thump 'em where it shows and in the second place, if your hand has slipped a bit, you just stick twice as much sticking plaster on your face as he's got on his and swear he attacked you. I should have thought even the rawest bloody recruit knew that.' MacGregor's face assumed a disapproving expression which enraged Dover still more. 'And I don't know what you're looking so bloody superior about,' he snapped. 'Nobody's asking you to soil your lily-white hands, are they?'

'No, sir.'

'Well, belt up then! If I had a decent sergeant I could rely on him backing me up, but I know better than to trust a namby-pamby, little Lord Fauntleroy, white-haired, mother's pet like you. You squeamish types, you get right up my nose, you really do! And I suppose you've been mucking around as usual all afternoon and got precisely nowhere?'

'Only negative evidence, I'm afraid, sir,' admitted Mac-Gregor, greatly relieved that the conversation had taken a different turn. 'The Perkings had a joint bank account with a balance of just under thirty pounds. I've been to all the insurance agents in the town and they're checking with their head offices but certainly none of the local branches has got any record of any life assurance at all on Mrs Perking. They're pretty certain that they would have been informed if Perking had tried to insure her elsewhere for any substantial sum. And I've checked round the neighbours again, sir, and if Cynthia Perking was having an affair with anybody he must have been the invisible man. So that rules those two motives out, sir.'

'Oh well,' said Dover, examining his tongue with great concentration in the dressing-table mirror, 'I'm not going to bust a gut over it. I'll have the truth straight from the horse's mouth tonight.' He chuckled. 'Even if I have to knock a few teeth out to get it!'

As things turned out Dover's patience was exhausted long before the witching hour of two a.m. By eleven o'clock he announced that he was blowed if a rotten little squirt like John Perking was going to keep him out of his bed any longer and sent MacGregor to phone for a taxi.

By half past eleven a sadistically smirking station sergeant had turfed Daniel Wibbley's unwanted son-in-law out of his bunk and conducted him to the more isolated of the two interviewing rooms. Out in the entrance hall Dover removed his overcoat and handed it to MacGregor.

'You wait here, laddie, and just see you remember what I told you. Nobody's to open that door until I ring the bell.'

The station sergeant led the way down the corridors. 'You won't be disturbing anybody down here, sir,' he told Dover with a knowing wink, 'no matter how loud you talk.'

'You've got the room arranged like I said?'

'That's right, sir. Just the one chair, nothing else. My, but this takes me back a bit, sir. The first sergeant I ever worked under – golly, he was a proper terror, he was! Got more free and voluntary confessions than the rest of the force put together. Fists like york hams, he had. He finished up as a night watchman at Wibbley's', he added soberly, 'after he got himself chucked out. Little Dan – that was this Mr Wibbley's father, sir – he was a great one for giving a chap a second chance. That way he didn't have to pay 'em standard wages, if you see what I mean. Well now, here we are, sir. I'll lock you in and the bell's just above the light switch by the door. I don't suppose you'll be long, will you, sir?'

'What', asked Dover with a snigger, 'do you think?'

John Perking had been waiting in the interview room for a good hour. It was icy cold and, in his shirtsleeves and stockinged feet, he was beginning to shiver. He was frightened, too. He had tried all his life to escape Canal Bank Street but it still haunted him in his dreams. The dirt. The poverty. The pub at the corner. Men and women alike screaming drunk on Saturday nights. The fights. The police. The bruises and the bandaged heads humorously compared in the light of the morning after. 'See that shiner, mate? It weren't you, mate, don't you flatter yourself! That bloody ginger-headed flattie give me that when I spewed out all over his bloody boots.' 'You should bloody worry, Jack! Come round t'corner and I'll show you what the lousy bastards did to me. They've had it in for me for weeks and I got a right going over. Five of 'em in a cell. Boots, bloody truncheons, the lot!'

Yes, all right, Perking told himself angrily as he rubbed his arms, that was Canal Bank Street. A running battle between the police and the yobbos who lived there. What else could you expect? But the new estate – Birdsfoot-Trefoil Close – that was different, surely? Respectable, law-abiding people who smiled and said good morning when they saw a copper. No policeman would dare lay a hand on them. And, damn it all, he still was Mr Wibbley's son-in-law, wasn't he? They'd have to use kid gloves when they handled him. They just wouldn't dare do anything else.

He leaned up against the white-washed wall and wiped the palms of his hands on his trousers.

His heart missed a beat. Footsteps outside. The sound of the door being unlocked. Opened. The big fat detective from London.

'Now look here,' said Perking, trying to keep his voice from soaring into a terrified soprano, 'I'd like to know what's going on.'

Dover eased his bowler hat back on his head and regarded his victim with interest. Miserable little runt. Scared pink, too. This shouldn't take long.

'I don't know why I've been dragged out of my bed in the middle of the night but you'd better get it clear right now that I'm not going to answer any questions. I know my rights. I don't have to say anything if I don't want to.'

Dover took a couple of leisurely menacing steps into the room. 'Oh, so you know your rights, do you? That's interesting. I didn't realize that we were dealing with an old lag. What were you up for last time, Perking?'

'I wasn't up for anything.'

'Oh, innocent were you? Well, we don't have to bother about little details like that this time, do we?'

Perking was about to speak again but thought better of it and clamped his mouth shut.

'Why don't you sit down, Perking?'

Perking looked round the room. There was just one spindly chair placed dead centre, directly under the light. 'I prefer to stand.'

'You're going to get very tired,' said Dover pleasantly. 'Unless, of course, you decide to be sensible and just answer a few simple questions.'

'I don't have to say anything if I don't want to,' repeated Perking doggedly.

'You're a proper little poll parrot, aren't you? Now then, why did you kill your wife?'

'I didn't.'

'Come off it, laddie! You killed her all right. You know

92

you did and I know you did so let's stop messing about. We know all about you trying to clean up in the kitchen after you'd bashed her head to a pulp in the front room. Very clever that was, but just not clever enough. If that's what you're relying on I should have another think about it if I were you.'

Perking was shaken. Even Dover could see that. His mouth sagged open incredulously and what colour was still left in his face ebbed away.

'Here,' – Dover turned on a kindly voice – 'you look as though you've had a bit of a shock. Come and sit down. You'll feel better in a minute or two.' He draped a fatherly arm round Perking's shoulders and escorted him to the chair.

'I'm all right,' mumbled Perking.

'Of course you are!' Dover smiled at him encouragingly. 'Now, just sit yourself down and take the load off your feet.'

Perking, his suspicions not entirely lulled, was inclined to resist, but Dover was pressing down heavily. Dover weighed seventeen and one quarter stone. Perking could manage ten and a half with his overcoat on. Dover leaned and Perking's legs bent at the knees.

He sat.

Or, at least, he would have sat if at the very last moment Dover had not, with beautiful timing, hooked the chair aside with his foot.

John Perking hit the floor hard in a painful and undignified sprawl. The chair toppled over and, being old and of inferior workmanship, collapsed into its component parts.

'My, my,' murmured Dover, oozing with sympathy, 'you are in a state, aren't you, laddie? What are you grovelling about down there for? No good trying to lick my boots, laddie. Things have gone a sight too far for that.' He bent down with a grunt and seized a fistful of Perking's hair. 'Oops-a-daisy!' Perking screamed as he was hauled roughly to his feet. 'Now, laddie,' leered Dover, maintaining his grip and jerking Perking's head methodically from side to side, 'feel more like talking, eh? I just want to know why you did her in, that's all.

Just give me a nice straight answer to a nice straight question and you and me, we'll be the best of friends, won't we?'

'You rotten, stinking, old swine!' shrieked Perking, trying to hack Dover's shins.

'Temper, temper!' chided Dover and administered a resounding slap across the face which brought tears to Perking's eyes. 'You want to be careful, laddie. I'm a very good-natured chap on the whole. I only start getting really nasty when I ask somebody a simple question and they won't give me a simple answer. Why did you kill your wife?'

'You can't bully me!' sobbed Perking.

'Oh, can't I? I shouldn't bet on it, laddie.' There was another yell of pain from Perking. Dover looked down. 'Sorry, laddie! Did I tread on your toes? I'll have to be more careful, won't I? Seeing as how you've got no shoes on. Now then — why did you kill your wife? You can tell me — I'm a married man myself.'

'I didn't kill her!' moaned Perking, writhing impotently in Dover's grasp.

Another hefty box across the ears. 'Don't contradict me, laddie! That gets me really mad, that does.'

'You go to hell!''

Dover began to get cross. If there was any justice in the world a weedy little specimen like Perking should have cracked at the first sniff of a bunched fist, but here he was, still on his feet and still breathing defiance. Dover raised his right hand and let Perking have it in the pit of the stomach. The young man doubled up and Dover, releasing his hold on the hair, speeded him on his way to the nearest wall with another resounding slap on the side of the head.

Perking hit the wall with his shoulder and sank, coughing and choking, on to his knees. Dover rubbed the knuckles of his right hand and prepared in his usual measured and majestic manner to continue the treatment.

Which is where the Chief Inspector made his mistake.

Perking was bruised and dazed, all right, but he was a deal tougher than Dover had given him credit for. He made a real effort and, with a howl of fury, launched himself off the wall before his tormentor could reach him. Perking might have swerved to the right or he might have swerved to the left. In actual fact like a panic-stricken mouse he plunged forward in a straight line and scored with his head a perfect bull's eye on Dover's advancing paunch. By pure chance he caught Dover at his most vulnerable.

' 'Strewth!' gasped Dover a split second before the impact deprived him temporarily of all power of speech and he thudded writhing on to the floor.

Perking, once having seized the initiative, had enough gumption not to rest on his laurels. Quick as lightning he grabbed the largest piece of the broken chair and proceeded with considerable relish to beat Dover round the head with it, having first knocked off the protective bowler hat.

The subsequent bellows could be heard quite distinctly all over the police station. MacGregor, sitting with the sergeant at his desk, cringed with shame. His companion, however, was visibly impressed.

'Cor,' he observed throatily, 'get a load of that! He's a lad, your Chief Inspector, all right! I wouldn't mind working with a chap like that, straight I wouldn't. At least you know where you are with him.'

'You do, indeed,' murmured MacGregor.

'Cor, listen to him! Here, I hope he doesn't kill the poor little bleeder.'

'So', agreed MacGregor with a shiver, 'do I.'

In the circumstances this total misinterpretation of what was happening in the interviewing room was understandable. The two sergeants continued to sit patiently in the front office while Dover, behind a solidly locked door, screamed first for help and then for mercy.

In a straight fight Dover would have won hands down, going on the principle that a bad big 'un will beat a bad little 'un any day. But Dover was labouring under two crucial disadvantages: unlike Perking, he wasn't armed and, also unlike Perking, he wasn't on his feet and thus able to make full use of his superior height and weight. Had he been left to himself there is no doubt that Dover would have eventually managed to achieve an upright position but the villain Perking, spinning around like a mini-dervish, resolutely refused to leave him alone. With his stout chair leg he incessantly whacked the fallen giant round the head and shoulders, varying his attack with an occasional poke in the stomach from the splintered end of his weapon. Dover cursed and feebly tried to beat off the mosquito-like onslaught.

MacGregor paused in the act of lighting yet another cigarette. 'Was that the Chief Inspector shouting for help?' he asked doubtfully.

'Course not!' scoffed the station sergeant. 'What would he be wanting help for? He's doing all right by himself from the sound of it. Do you feel like a cup of tea?'

MacGregor listened again and then shrugged his shoulders. 'Yes, that sounds a good idea. I suppose he'll ring the bell if he wants us.'

'Course he will,' agreed the station sergeant, going to fill the kettle in the gents.

The bell. It was Dover's last hope of salvation. The only trouble was that he couldn't reach it. Perking was still thrashing enthusiastically away and stamping as hard as he could on Dover's hands whenever it looked as though the Chief Inspector was going to drag himself to his feet. If Dover had not been so grossly overweight or if he had not been the most out-of-condition police officer north and south of a line drawn from the Wash to the Bristol Channel, the disgraceful farce might have been ended sooner. As it was, Dover had to wait until John Perking was just too exhausted to hit him any more.

At long last the bell rang.

MacGregor jumped to his feet. 'Thank God!' he said with relief. 'Come on, let's get 'em out of there! I just hope the stupid old fool hasn't gone too far this time.'

The two sergeants stared unbelievingly through the open door of the interviewing room.

MacGregor, he of the razor-sharp reactions and the big feet, got the first words out. 'Quick, fetch a doctor!'

Dover, slumped by the door with two black eyes and blood pouring down his face, groaned. 'No, you bloody fool!' he mumbled through swollen lips, so indistinctly that nobody understood him.

Chapter Eight

'It's all your blasted fault!' insisted Dover viciously. 'Why the blazes you had to go dragging in that bloody doctor is beyond me. Anybody'd think', he added, squinting suspiciously out of two unlovely black eyes, 'that you were deliberately trying to shop me.'

'Oh, sir!' protested MacGregor and endeavoured to look as though the thought had never ever crossed his mind.

'And that damned magistrate,' Dover grumbled on. 'Fat old cow! They shouldn't allow women on the bench, I've always said so. No judgment, women. And they don't know when to keep their traps shut.'

'Are you ready for your sweet, sir?'

'What is it?'

'Apple dumplings, sir.'

'Well,' said Dover grudgingly, 'I'll try and force a few mouthfuls down.' He handed over his dirty plate, which looked as though it had received a visitation from a plague of locusts.

MacGregor stacked it tidily on the tray on the dressing-table and ladled out a massive helping of apple dumpling. 'Is that enough, sir?'

Dover scowled at it. 'It'll do for a start.'

Nearly two whole days had passed since the incident in the interviewing room and Dover was now beginning to sit up and take notice. Sustenance he had been partaking of all along as, luckily, his appetite had not been impaired. He shovelled down the apple dumpling but he was not in the sunniest of moods.

' "Why has the accused got that piece of sticking plaster on his cheek?" ' he piped, imitating, as MacGregor (who had been through this sixteen times already) knew only too well, the female magistrate. 'Silly cow! It's a pity they didn't let me get a word in. I'd have told her a few home truths instead of yes-your-worshipping and no-your-worshipping all over the damned place.'

In the magistrates' court itself Dover had had to play a non-speaking role. It was Inspector Mansion who had risen, rather unwillingly, to his feet and explained to the Bench that the prisoner had attacked a police officer during questioning and had had to be restrained. 'Only', said Inspector Mansion, 'a reasonable amount of force was used.'

The Bench, led by the female magistrate, was sceptical.

A heavily bandaged Dover was produced as evidence.

The female magistrate was scathing. Did the police really expect them to believe that a great hulking brute like Dover had been assaulted and beaten up by the weak and tiny prisoner? The idea was ludicrous! She would like to remind Inspector Mansion that she had been sitting on this Bench, woman and girl, for thirty-five years and she was well aware that thick bandages and sticking plaster on policemen more often concealed disgraceful breaches of the Judges' Rules than genuine injuries. She was, she was sure, speaking for her brother magistrates when she warned that such flagrant examples of police brutality would not be tolerated in Pott Winckle, that well-known cradle of civil liberty. The police had been warned and had better not let it occur again.

Dover's attempts to speak up for truth and justice were speedily thwarted by his colleagues and he had been removed bodily from the well of the court before he got himself booked for gross contempt. The rank injustice of the whole episode had left him with a burning resentment against women J.P.s and a fierce determination to get John Perking by hook or by crook.

'He'll rue the day he was born,' threatened Dover, licking the last of the custard off his spoon. 'I'll teach him it doesn't pay to start crossing swords with me.'

MacGregor fetched the cheese and biscuits. During the past forty-eight hours he had been trying to persuade the Chief Inspector that he could now safely retire from the case with honour. His wounds alone entitled him to that. The murderer had been found and any loose ends which still needed tying up could be tied up by MacGregor himself. But, in spite of a life-long devotion to lead-swinging, Dover wasn't having any. For the moment he was now as vehement as Daniel Wibbley him-self that Perking should be made to suffer the full rigours of the law. Nothing was too bad for that little rat.

'He's not going to wriggle out of this one,' snarled Dover, spattering crumbs all over the sheets. 'He's going to rot behind bars for the rest of his life – and I hope he lives to be a hundred. I'll fix him, the bastard! Now, you've got it all clear, have you, MacGregor? Tomorrow morning we'll go and see this Topping-Wibbley chap and get him out of the way. Once we've established his innocence for good and all we'll start on uncovering Perking's motive for the murder. It shouldn't be too difficult if we put our backs into it. And no mucking about with kid gloves, either, this time. This time I mean business. Where's my coffee?'

'Here you are, sir.'

'You've ordered the Rolls-Royce for ten o'clock, have you?'

'Yes, sir.'

'And fixed up about the chair?'

'Yes, sir. We're borrowing one from the local hospital.'

'Good. Well, you can push off now. I don't want to see you again till dinner-time. I've got to try and preserve my strength. And tell 'em not to be so skinny with the spuds tonight.'

Dover in a wheelchair was a sight to reduce strong men to tears. He clung terrified to the arms and shouted curses and instructions over his shoulder at MacGregor who was entrusted with the task of pushing. Since all Dover's injuries were super-ficial and restricted to his head and shoulders there was really no reason why he couldn't have walked perfectly well, but the Chief Inspector believed in getting his money's worth.

Mr and Mrs Topping-Wibbley lived well outside Pott Winckle, and up wind of it, in a large and expensive house standing in its own grounds. MacGregor was favourably im-pressed as he wheeled Dover up to the front door.

'Don't go so damned fast!' squawked Dover. 'You'll be tipping me over if you don't look out. You'd think people'd have enough consideration to keep their paths smooth, wouldn't you? And when we get in there, you ask the questions. I'll only chip in if I feel like it. Get it?'

Mr and Mrs Topping-Wibbley, having been warned of the visit by telephone, were awaiting their guests in the drawing-room. Dover was wheeled across to a cosy position by the fire.

The Topping-Wibbleys sat side by side on an enormous, zebra-striped settee and stared in some amazement at their august visitor. They were overawed by this devotion beyond and above the call of duty.

MacGregor cleared his throat loudly. The Topping-Wibbleys dragged their eyes away and looked at him.

'Well,' began MacGregor, snapping open his notebook, 'I expect you know why we're here?'

Mrs Topping-Wibbley answered. She usually did. 'If it's about that dreadful Perking man, I'm afraid we can't help you. If I'd answered the telephone when you rang I could have told you that and saved you the trouble of the journey. We had nothing to do with Perking at all. In fact, I've never actually spoken to him in my life. We've had nothing to do with Cynthia either since she married him. I quite liked Cynthia, but the way she treated poor Uncle Daniel — well, we thought that was quite unforgivable. All but broke his heart, she did. Only people who are close to him, like Hereward and I, know what her behaviour did to poor Uncle Daniel. That's right, isn't it, darling?'

'Yes, darling,' said Mr Topping-Wibbley.

'One doesn't like to speak ill of the dead, sergeant, but one can't help feeling that this was a judgment on Cynthia. I know it's supposed to be old-fashioned but it does tell you in the Bible to honour your father and mother, doesn't it? I can't think what came over Cynthia. Uncle Daniel was devoted to her and she had a lovely home and everything. And now look where she is! Poor Uncle Daniel — it's him I feel sorry for. We've been doing our best, Hereward and I, to try and make it up to him.

He relies very heavily on my husband – doesn't he, darling? Of course they work very closely together in the business and that makes an additional bond. They have their little disagreements, naturally, but whatever you've heard you can take my word for it – they're just storms in teacups. Even business partners can't be expected to see eye-to-eye over every tiny detail, can they?'

'Business partners?' queried MacGregor. 'I didn't know you were Mr Wibbley's business partner, sir.'

'Well, not in name, of course,' said Mrs Topping-Wibbley smoothly. 'Naturally a young man like Hereward doesn't jump in right at the top of a big concern like that, even if he is the boss's nephew. People get so stupidly jealous, you know. No, Hereward started right at the bottom, just like any other bright young man with a brilliant future ahead of him. And we think it's the only fair way, don't we, darling?'

'Yes, darling,' said Mr Topping-Wibbley.

'What precisely is your position in the firm, sir?' asked MacGregor.

'Well, at the moment he's Assistant Sales Manager,' said Mrs Topping-Wibbley with a bright laugh. 'It's a very important job, really. Of course, he's moving about all the time. Uncle Daniel keeps a very fatherly eye on his progress – doesn't he, darling? As he gets a bit more experience so he gets a bit more responsibility.'

Dover stopped watching the flickering electric flames and looked at Mrs Topping-Wibbley. Then he looked at Mr Topping-Wibbley and sniffed, audibly.

MacGregor broke what was promising to turn into a rather embarrassing silence. 'I suppose the death of Cynthia Perking will make a great difference to your prospects, won't it, sir?'

Mrs Topping-Wibbley proved capable of taking a hint. With a triumphant glance at Dover she let her husband answer for himself.

'Er – I don't quite know what you mean,' he stammered awkwardly.

'Oh, darling, it's perfectly obvious what the sergeant means!

And you're quite wrong, too, sergeant!' She shook her head at MacGregor in playful reproach. 'Cynthia would never have taken any part in the running of the business, whatever had happened. Uncle Daniel is a firm believer in the principle that a woman's place is in the home. He would never allow any woman, even his own daughter, to become head of the business. It was always intended that my husband would succeed his uncle there.'

'But Mrs Perking would presumably have inherited the actual ownership of the firm?'

'Well, probably, but we weren't anticipating any difficulty in that direction,' said Mrs Topping-Wibbley. 'Hereward would have been managing director and Cynthia would just have been majority shareholder, that's all.'

'And now your husband will be both?'

'Good heavens!' Mrs Topping-Wibbley switched on the bright smile again. 'That's all very far in the future, we hope. We have no idea how Uncle Daniel will dispose of his shares now, have we, darling?'

'No,' said Mr Topping-Wibbley through taut lips.

'Did you know Cynthia Perking was going to have a baby, sir?' asked MacGregor suddenly. He had a feeling that the interview was beginning to get bogged down and that if he didn't get a move on Dover would barge in and take over.

'Not until last night,' Mrs Topping-Wibbley said, climbing automatically once again into the saddle. 'That just makes it all the more horrible, doesn't it? Poor Uncle Daniel, he was so longing for a grandson. Oh well,' she laughed softly, 'he'll just have to make do with our three boisterous offspring now, won't he, darling? Poor man, I suppose we're all the family he's really got left now.'

'He has got a sister and a wife,' Mr Topping-Wibbley pointed out rather disagreeably.

'Yes, but you know what I mean, darling!' His wife bared her teeth at him in a fair imitation of indulgence.

'To get back to what we were talking about ... ' MacGregor plunged in again, thus earning full marks for trying ' ... you didn't know, sir, before she was murdered that Cynthia Perking was pregnant?'

Mr Topping-Wibbley shook his head.

'She didn't tell you, sir, when you called on her shortly before she died?'

There was a moment's hesitation while the implications of MacGregor's question sank in and then an outburst of well-bred indignation.

'I haven't the least idea what you're talking about,' protested Mr Topping-Wibbley. 'I haven't seen Cynthia since before her marriage.'

'Are you trying to suggest that my husband had anything even remotely to do with Cynthia's murder?' stormed his wife. 'I've never heard anything so ridiculous in my life! You evidently don't know my husband. He isn't capable of harming a fly.'

MacGregor sat calmly through it all and, when the Topping-Wibbleys finally ran out of breath, went on with his questions. 'Am I to take it, sir, that you deny going to see your cousin, Cynthia Perking, on the afternoon she was killed?'

'Well, of course he denies it. Hereward, for God's sake, don't just sit there like a dummy! Can't you see how their minds are working? Sergeant, I can't imagine why you have come here asking such ridiculous questions but I can tell you here and now that I refuse to have my husband implicated in the death of Cynthia Perking. This matter can be cleared up in a couple of seconds. In the first place, in deference to Uncle Daniel's wishes, neither Hereward nor I have had anything to do with Cynthia since she married that dreadful little man. And, in the second place, my husband wasn't even in Pott Winckle on the day of her death. He spent the greater part of the day over at Breadford and he didn't get back home until after seven o'clock.'

MacGregor looked somewhat crestfallen. 'Is that true, sir?'

'Course it is!' rumbled Dover, creaking irritably in his wheel-chair. 'I told you all along you were barking up a gum tree. The chap's got an alibi. Not that it matters a damn one way or the other.'

'What do you mean – it doesn't matter?' demanded Mrs Topping-Wibbley.

'The afternoon caller, whoever he was, didn't kill Cynthia Perking,' explained Dover through an enormous yawn. 'Her husband did.'

MacGregor was furious at this gratuitous intervention. A fat chance you had of trying to be subtle when Dover was around! He tried to salvage something from the wreck.

'Well, there you are, sir,' he said, turning back to Mr Topping-Wibbley. 'The Chief Inspector has given you the official point of view so, if you did call to see Mrs Perking, there's absolutely no reason why you shouldn't tell us, is there, sir? It's just a matter of helping us build up a clear and accurate picture of her last hours.'

Mr Topping-Wibbley was still looking unhappy. 'I didn't go to see Cynthia,' he repeated.

'Why on earth', asked his help-mate, 'should you think he did?'

'We've had a description of the caller, madam, and it does fit your husband.'

'And half the male population of the country, too,' growled Dover.

'And', continued MacGregor, ignoring the interruption, 'we do have a description of his car.'

Mrs Topping-Wibbley relaxed. 'That old Bugatti of his? Well, sergeant, I'm afraid that somebody's been leading you up the garden path. There are a lot of people in the town who are antagonistic towards us – little jealous people, you know, working class and socialists and things like that – but I never thought that they'd go to these lengths to embarrass us. However, on this occasion their maliciousness has gone completely astray. On the day that Cynthia died it so happens that my husband's Bugatti was out of action in our garage with carburettor trouble. Hereward borrowed my car to go to Breadford in.'

MacGregor could hardly believe his luck. It just showed what he could do if only he were given the chance. 'Is your car a dark-green M.G. 1100, madam? This year's registration?'

Mrs Topping-Wibbley stared at him. 'Yes,' she said slowly.

'That's the description of the car we were given, madam.'

Mrs Topping-Wibbley turned to look at her husband. He was studiously examining his shoes and didn't return her glance.

'Hereward,' said Mrs Topping-Wibbley sharply, 'you did go to Breadford, didn't you?'

'Of course I did,' he muttered uncomfortably. 'Good heavens, there must be thousands of those M.G.s knocking around. Why try and involve me, for heaven's sake?'

'We have to explore all the avenues, sir,' MacGregor pointed out urbanely.

'Well, this one is quite clearly a cul-de-sac,' retorted Mr Topping-Wibbley with a sudden burst of spirit. 'I'm very sorry, sergeant, but I obviously can't help you. And now, if that's all, I really must ask you to excuse me. I have to be getting in to the office.' He stood up.

MacGregor didn't budge. 'Breadford, I think you said, sir?' He flicked over to a clean page in his notebook. 'Could you tell me what time you left to get there?'

'For God's sake!' Mr Topping-Wibbley sat down again with a gesture of impatience. 'Is all this really necessary?'

'I'm afraid so, sir. We'd just like to check.'

Mr Topping-Wibbley flung an uneasy glance at his wife. 'I left here at about eleven o'clock in the morning and I drove straight to Breadford. I had some work I could be getting on with at home so I didn't bother going into the office. Coming back, I left Breadford at about six and got back home about a quarter past seven. My wife and the au pair girl will no doubt be able to confirm that. They told me that Cynthia had been killed as soon as I got in and, naturally, I went round to Uncle Daniel's right away to see if there was anything I could do.'

'And the purpose of your visit to Breadford, sir?'

'I went on business.'

'I'm afraid I shall have to ask you to be more explicit, sir. If you could just give me the names and addresses of the people you saw in Breadford ... '

'Damn it all!' exploded Mr Topping-Wibbley, getting, to MacGregor's great satisfaction, more and more hunted-looking. 'Do you have to go on like this? I suppose if I start giving you names and addresses you'll go round asking questions, won't you. Well, it just so happens, sergeant, that I don't like being treated as a criminal and I don't choose to have my friends harried and questioned by the police.'

MacGregor was all but licking his lips with delighted anticipation. If he hadn't hit the jack-pot this time, he'd eat his hat! Innocent men didn't in the least bit mind involving their friends to prove their innocence. He got ready to subject Mr Topping-Wibbley to another dose of delicate needling when, once again, the scarlet lips of Mrs Topping-Wibbley parted.

'Don't be a fool, Hereward!' she snapped. 'You must forgive my husband, sergeant, but the truth of the matter is that when he went to Breadford he was really practically playing truant and, naturally, he'd prefer Uncle Daniel not to know about it. You do understand, don't you? My husband is a fanatic about these dreadful old cars and he's got a crony in Breadford. They get together whenever they can and talk about pinions and ratchets and all that sort of thing. Hereward's friend is the manager of one of our big storage warehouses in Breadford, so my husband has a bit of an excuse for popping over there once in a while. Naturally he's no reason for spending the whole day there and that's why he's a bit touchy about what time he got there and when he left. Now this manager's name is Tony Geddes and you'll find him at Wibbley's Main Storage Depot in Breadford.'

'Thank you, madam.'

Mr Topping-Wibbley glared sulkily at Mrs Topping-Wibbley and chewed his bottom lip at the same time.

'Right!' said Dover, spurred on by the first pangs of hunger. 'Well, that's that. We won't bother you any longer. Come on, MacGregor!'

He was halfway across the room before anybody, including himself, remembered that he'd arrived in a wheelchair.

Chapter Nine

FOR once Chief Inspector Dover didn't retire to bed immediately after lunch. To tell the truth, he was getting thoroughly bored with his hotel bedroom and, since the weather had taken an unexpected turn for the better, he had come to the conclusion that a little trip out into the country would do his health a world of good. If one has a chauffeur-driven Rolls-Royce at one's disposal, why not use it?

MacGregor was far from pleased at the prospect of having Dover's dead weight tied once again round his neck. Exasperating as Dover's habit was of doing no work at all after midday, it was better than having his constant interference in matters which a younger and better man could handle far more efficiently. Of course, MacGregor had long since reached the stage in his relationship with Dover in which nothing that the old bungler did was right. Still, as MacGregor had been told several times by the Assistant Commissioner, he wasn't in the police to enjoy himself.

'I hope', observed Dover, idly scraping with a grubby fingernail at a spot of grease on his bowler hat, 'you don't still think this Topping-Wibbley fellow's got anything to do with the murder?'

'Well, I wasn't over-impressed by his demeanour this morning, were you, sir? I thought he looked very shifty. If you ask me, he's hiding something.'

'With a wife like that, who wouldn't? He ought to have given her a good belt round the ears years ago. I'd like to see my old woman taking the words out of my mouth like that, by golly I would!'

'That dark-green car,' said MacGregor, 'you can't get away from that, can you, sir?'

'You've got to make it clear right from the start' – Dover stared blearily out of the window – 'who's boss. If you don't, you're sunk.'

'If it wasn't his car parked in Birdsfoot-Trefoil Close, it's an amazing coincidence, sir, isn't it?' MacGregor watched the passing countryside through his window.

'If a man isn't master in his own house,' asked Dover, 'what is he? You've just got to put your foot down, that's all. And put it down firmly. If her toes get in the way, hard bloody luck!'

'As I see it,' mused MacGregor, 'he decides to go and call on his cousin Cynthia for some reason or another. Maybe he's heard somehow that she's going to have a baby? Well, that doesn't matter for the moment. But, whatever his reason was, he was trying to do it on the q.t. He puts his own car out of action because anybody in the town would recognize it, and borrows his wife's.'

'Course, marriage is a big mistake, a big mistake. It's the women who want to get married, not the men. Men have more damned sense.'

'That means the visit, at any rate, was premeditated. Premeditated and surreptitious. And on the very day she's found murdered. Well, if that doesn't sound suspicious, I don't know what does. Don't you agree, sir?'

'Eh?' said Dover crossly.

'Topping-Wibbley's behaviour on the day of the murder, sir?'

'Are you still rabbiting on about that?' grumbled Dover. 'You can't see the wood for the trees, that's your trouble. I don't care two flipping hoots what Topping-Wibbley did or what he didn't do. Perking murdered his wife and if you think anybody else did you're a bigger nit than I gave you credit for. Look, laddie, give it a rest, will you? Topping-Wibbley wasn't anywhere near Birdsfoot-Trefoil Close. He was seeing this What's-his-name fellow at Where-is-it. If it hadn't been such a nice day and if I hadn't thought the drive might do me good we wouldn't be wasting our time sitting here now. Get it?'

'Well, sir,' said MacGregor reprovingly, 'I do think we'd have done better to get on to this Tony Geddes by phone the moment we left the Topping-Wibbleys' house. By the time we get to Breadford they'll have had time to cook up half-a-dozen phoney alibis between them.'

'Fiddlesticks!' snorted Dover. 'Topping-Wibbley doesn't need any perishing alibi and, if he did, he'd have fixed it up days ago, wouldn't he?'

'Possibly, sir.'

Dover sniffed. 'If he was planning murder, he'd be a damned fool if he didn't.'

Tony Geddes was a good-natured-looking young man with a frank and open face. Dover took an immediate dislike to him, a fact which was, if anything, slightly in his favour. Geddes welcomed Dover and MacGregor into his office, sat them down in a couple of comfortable chairs and announced that two cups of the liquid that cheers but does not inebriate would be along toot sweet.

'Know it's against the rules to offer you boys in blue any of the hard stuff,' he chortled merrily.

MacGregor had been very careful. He had simply asked if Messrs Dover and MacGregor could see Mr Geddes for a few minutes on a matter of some urgency. It was not exactly a dishonest approach.

'How did you know we were policemen, Mr Geddes?' he asked politely after a brief what-did-I-tell-you glance at Dover.

Tony Geddes's mouth dropped open. 'Eh? Oh. Well, didn't my little bit of office work outside say ... ?'

'No,' said MacGregor, 'she didn't.'

'Oh? Well, you must just look like a brace of rozzers, eh? Big feet, you know, and all that razamataz!' He laughed heartily.

Dover and MacGregor preserved a stony silence. References to the size of policemen's feet did not amuse them.

'After all, you are policemen, aren't you?'

'Yes,' said MacGregor.

'Well, it was a good guess then, wasn't it?'

'Or prior information, sir.'

Tony Geddes's face creased in hurt bewilderment. He managed to produce another insouciant laugh. 'I can see I'd better keep my trap shut before I put the old foot in it, eh?'

'I suppose Mr Topping-Wibbley did phone you that we were on our way, sir?'

'Eh? No, no, of course he didn't. I don't know what you're talking about.' Tony Geddes got very red.

'I'm sorry, sir, but I was under the impression that he was a friend of yours.'

'Well,' – defiantly – 'he is.'

'And he didn't warn you that we were coming? That wasn't very friendly of him, was it, sir? Well, I'm sorry, sir. I'd have phoned you myself but I felt sure that Mr Topping-Wibbley would have let you know.'

Tony Geddes wriggled miserably. Now he didn't know what to say. Dover watched his discomfort with something approaching approval. That young whippersnapper Mac-Gregor was learning. You had to grant him that. Quite a text-book little lesson, really, in how to deal with members of the public.

Tony Geddes slowly wet his lips. 'Er – to what do I owe the pleasure of this visit anyhow?'

MacGregor's eyebrows shot up in most convincing surprise. 'Well, we were really expecting you to give us some information, sir.'

Tony Geddes began to sweat. What the hell did that mean? Then his face cleared. He'd show 'em he wasn't as big a fool as he looked. 'Oh, you've come about the pilfering, have you? We always have a certain amount of it but, just recently, it seems to have been getting a touch out of hand.'

'Two detectives from Scotland Yard to investigate petty pilfering, sir?' MacGregor shook his head in quite a kindly manner.

Tony Geddes cleared his throat.

'Did you say something, sir?'

Tony Geddes shook his head.

Dover joined in the fun. 'Mr Geddes isn't being very co-operative, is he, sergeant? Pity, that. I just hope he doesn't come to regret it.'

'Look here,' — Tony Geddes appealed desperately to them — 'I didn't want to get involved in all this in the first place.'

'Didn't you, sir?' MacGregor's tone was sceptical.

'No, I didn't. And Hereward Topping-Wibbley has no damned right to bring my name into it. I'm the last chap to jib at giving a pal a helping hand, but murder's getting a bit too deep for yours truly. And I don't care if his uncle *is* the head of the firm. This isn't the only job in the world, not by a long piece of chalk it isn't.' He glared indignantly around his office. 'I've been thinking about cutting adrift for quite a while now.'

MacGregor caught Dover's eye and winked. He couldn't resist it. After all, he'd been so right, hadn't he? This alibi of Hereward Topping-Wibbley's obviously wasn't worth the breath it had been spoken with and he, MacGregor, had been saying that all along. Perhaps the next time the Chief Inspector would pay a little more attention to his opinions. If MacGregor had been a mite less cock-a-hoop at his own cleverness he might have noticed that Dover's expression was not one of benevolent encouragement.

Tony Geddes was blithely ignorant of the barely declared war which was continually raging between Dover and MacGregor. He, poor soul, just wanted to confess and it was just too bad if he shopped Hereward Topping-Wibbley and ruined Dover's day in the process. Some people are very selfish.

'Look,' he said, turning eagerly to MacGregor, 'I think I'd better tell you exactly what happened.'

'It might be a good idea,' MacGregor agreed dryly.

'Well, Hereward gave me a tinkle — oh, one day last week some time — and said would I do the old boy-scout act and cover up for him. He wanted to get away from the office one afternoon and would I alibi him. He didn't want either his wife or the Big Boss to know about it. Well, naturally, I thought he'd found himself a popsie somewhere – and if you'd met his trouble and strife you wouldn't think that too out of the ordinary. Well, I said I would. What else could I do? Hereward's by way of being a bit of a chum of mine and it's well on the cards that he might be my boss one day. A chap's got to think of his future, hasn't he? I don't want to spend the rest of my life checking how many lavatory chains we've got in stock. I'm not one to toot the old trombone but I reckon I'm cut out for something a bit better than that. Well, Hereward was very grateful and said he'd do likewise for me one fine day and I said, no, I didn't fancy these oriental types – all quite innocent chiff-chaff, you see. Well, we fixed up what I'd say and everything, if anybody phoned when he was supposed to be here, and that was that. He said thanks a billion and I said don't mench and if you can't be good – be original. I didn't think any more about it. Nobody did phone up for him so I didn't have to perjure the old immortal. And even when I heard that old Wibbley's daughter had been murdered, the tanner didn't drop. I just assumed this queer husband type of hers did it, especially when you bottles of blue turned the key on him.'

'What's made you revise your opinion?'

'Well, Hereward rang me up just before nosh-time today and sort of said he'd had the cops round and I was going to be decent and stick by his phoney alibi, wasn't I? Well, that sent a shiver down the old vertebrae, I can tell you! But well, like I said, I've got to keep on the sunny side of old Hereward, so I agreed. I feel a double-dyed-in-the-wool tea-caddy about spilling the old beans now but – hell's ringing bells – I don't want to be an accessory before and after, do I? A chap's got to look after his own epidermis, hasn't he?'

'What makes you so sure Topping-Wibbley is a murderer?' demanded Dover furiously.

Tony Geddes clutched his big red ears and twisted them in anguish. 'Oh God, you don't mean to say that he didn't kill her after all? He's never going to forgive me for this, never. It's going to be the big chopper for Tony boy, but quick. Fetch me the labour exchange! Well, naturally I assumed you'd got your eagle eye on him — or else why the blue blazes are you here?'

'Just routine,' said Dover, looking grumpy. 'John Perking killed his wife, that's for sure. Nobody's any doubts about that.' A black scowl in MacGregor's direction. 'But there was some damned fool woman who claimed she'd seen somebody like Hereward Topping-Wibbley calling at the Perkings' house. Load of old cod's wallop, of course, but in our job you've got to check these things. We spend three quarters of our time', he grumbled, 'following up the damned-fool things the general public tells us. So there you are — nobody's accusing your friend of murder. If he'd told us properly where he was that afternoon we shouldn't have come haring off here on a wild-goose chase. Some people have no damned consideration. You can see the state I'm in, can't you? All got in the line of duty, too. I ought to be in bed now, that's where I ought to be. Not that anyone gives you any thanks for it.' He lapsed into a moody silence.

'Er — quite,' said Tony Geddes.

MacGregor closed his notebook and put it away in his pocket. 'And you've no idea where Mr Topping-Wibbley was on the afternoon in question, sir?'

Tony Geddes shook his head. 'No, he didn't say a dicky-bird. Look — all this business has put me in a bit of an old fix, hasn't it? Do you have to let Hereward know that I split on him? It's going to make it damned awkward for me.'

'I'm afraid we shall have to ask Mr Topping-Wibbley where he actually was, sir.'

'Oh, hell!' said Tony Geddes, looking very worried. 'Oh, hell! Of all the lousy luck!'

MacGregor could hardly agree. In his opinion hard work, conscientiousness and a natural flair were paying off in a big way, and he was eager to be up and off on a trail which was hotting up nicely. He turned to Dover. 'Well, I don't think we need take up any more of Mr Geddes's time, do you, sir?'

Dover answered the question with a look of undisguised loathing.

'Shall we be going, sir?' asked MacGregor hopefully.

'Not until I've had that cup of tea, laddie.'

In spite of an atmosphere which was rather impregnated with embarrassment, Dover had his cup of tea. It was the one bright spot in an otherwise dreary day. He didn't even enjoy the drive back to Pott Winckle much. Rolls-Royces aren't all that special once you get used to them, and the chauffeur, in spite of Dover's continual remonstrances, would keep tearing along at thirty-five miles an hour. And then there was MacGregor, bubbling over like cheap champagne. Dover gritted his teeth and stuck pig-headedly to his guns. He was more determined than ever to pin this murder on John Perking. And, as he told himself, not without reason. Daniel Wibbley wanted it, Dover's own acute injuries cried aloud for vengeance and – Dover frowned. Damn it all, there was another reason, he could swear there was. Oh yes, Perking was guilty.

MacGregor was chattering happily away. 'I expect Geddes got on the blower to his chum Hereward the moment we left his office, don't you, sir? That'll put the wind up Topping-Wibbley all right. What do you think, sir – should we storm round and grill him right away or should we let him sweat it out till morning?' MacGregor chuckled and rubbed his hands in joyful anticipation.

'You're a right little sadist, you are and no mistake,' said Dover. 'Hounding an innocent man – it's a crying shame! Well, watch it, laddie, that's all. One step out of line and I'll drop on you like a ton of bricks.'

'But we will have to interview Topping-Wibbley again, sir, won't we?'

'Tomorrow, maybe,' grunted Dover.

'Oh, but I've just remembered, sir, we'll have to attend the inquest on Cynthia Perking tomorrow. On balance, sir, I really think it might be better to confront Topping-Wibbley tonight. We could go straight round now, sir, while we've still got the car, couldn't we?'

'No,' said Dover. 'I'll thank you to remember that this is my first day up from a sick bed. I'm not made of iron, you know. Even I can't go on for ever.'

'No, sir,' said MacGregor dolefully.

The Rolls drew up outside the entrance to the hotel.

MacGregor's face broke into a wide smile. The unmistakable Type 51 Bugatti of Hereward Topping-Wibbley was parked just ahead of them.

Dover heaved himself up with a groan on to his bed. 'Bloody liberty!' he growled. 'Of all the nerve!' He flopped back weakly on to the pillows. 'Stop in bed and rest, that's what the doctor told me.' He rose up on one elbow and glowered at Hereward Topping-Wibbley out of yellowing black eyes. 'Fat chance I get!'

Topping-Wibbley sat down firmly on a chair. 'Well, I'm very sorry and all that,' he said with a callousness that cut Dover to the quick, 'but I want this mess straightened out here and now.'

'I'm a martyr to my stomach,' murmured Dover, rolling uneasily from side to side. 'It's all the nervous tension. Take it easy, that's what the specialist said.' He gazed mournfully at the ceiling. 'The irony of it!'

'I understand that Tony Geddes told you that I didn't go to Breadford on the day Cynthia was killed?'

'He did,' agreed MacGregor shortly. 'And before you try any more cock-and-bull stories on us, Topping-Wibbley, I think I should warn you that giving the police misleading and erroneous information is a very serious matter. We are investigating a murder case and you have placed yourself in a very invidious situation. If you'll take my advice you'll be perfectly frank with us now and … '

'Oh, shut up!' snarled Dover, sitting up and trying to reach his boot laces. 'Don't take any notice of him.' He addressed Mr Topping-Wibbley. 'He knows as well as I do that you didn't do her in. Nipped off for a bit of the old slap-and-tickle, did you? Well, we're all men of the world here. Nothing you say'll go beyond these four walls so spit it out.'

'Just a minute, sir,' – MacGregor couldn't let this pass – 'whatever Mr Topping-Wibbley has to tell us will have to be checked. However, we will be as discreet about it as possible but we can't promise more than that.'

'If', said Hereward Topping-Wibbley through tight lips, 'you would be so good as to let me get a word in edgeways, I should be very pleased to make a statement. I want to get this over with as quickly as possible. I shall have enough trouble explaining my absence to my wife as it is.'

'Well, you should have thought of that before, shouldn't you, laddie?' said Dover, leering salaciously.

'Chief Inspector, I have not been deceiving my wife! Will you kindly refrain from making these unpleasant insinuations. They are insulting not only to me but to Mrs Topping-Wibbley as well.'

' 'Strewth!' muttered Dover and turned his face to the wall.

'Sergeant,' – Mr Topping-Wibbley turned to address his sole remaining audience – 'I think you are pretty well aware of my position in my uncle's business. Whatever Mrs Topping-Wibbley may imply, my life is not a bed of roses nor, at least until Cynthia's death, were my prospects exactly brilliant. I'm nothing more than a highly paid office boy, and shall be until Uncle Daniel is bricked up in the family vault. Even when that happy event takes place my troubles are by no means over. Cynthia would, in the normal course of time, have inherited the firm and heaven alone knows what she would have done. I had a strong suspicion that she wouldn't have found any place for me.'

'So you decided to kill her?' MacGregor prompted helpfully.

'Of course he didn't!' Dover rolled over again. 'Stop trying to put words in the poor devil's mouth!'

'Thank you, Chief Inspector. It's a great relief to find that not all policemen are sadistic bullies. No, the idea of murdering my cousin never for one moment crossed my mind. I tried to effect a much less dramatic solution. I explored the possibilities of getting another job.'

'Is that *all*?' demanded Dover, his former benevolence taking a severe shock.

'It may not sound much to you ... '

'It certainly doesn't!'

' ... but you can take my word for it, it was no simple undertaking for me.'

'The missus?'

'And my uncle. Neither of them would ever forgive me. My uncle would sling me out on my ear without a second's hesitation and my wife — well, I shudder to think what my wife would say, or do. She thinks that the sun rises and sets over Wibbley's sanitary fittings. So, you see, if I was going to make the break I had to present the pair of them with a fait accompli.' He looked doubtfully at Dover to see if this last erudite phrase had been understood. Since Dover was now lying flat on his back with his eyes closed and his mouth open, it was not easy to tell just how much was sinking in. Mr Topping-Wibbley shrugged his shoulders and went on with his story. 'So, without breathing a word to a living soul, I rang up the managing director of March and Jays.'

'March and Jays?' asked MacGregor.

'Our biggest rivals. Their stuff's slightly more expensive than ours and not so shoddy. My uncle speaks of them as having cornered the carriage trade. It's his idea of a joke. Actually there's nothing funny about the competition between us and them. It's anything goes and no holds barred. You can see why I had to keep the whole thing a deadly secret.' He laughed shortly. 'I even arranged my interview under a false name. However, Curtis — the managing director — he knew me all right when he saw me and he'll vouch that I was in his office from just after lunch until five o'clock. Here's his business card, if you're going to get in touch with him.'

With a crestfallen countenance MacGregor accepted the slip of pasteboard. Damn, damn, damn, and damn!

Dover yawned and scratched his head. 'Well, that's that,

isn't it? I thought there must be some perfectly innocent explanation. By the way, did you get the job?'

Hereward Topping-Wibbley slumped a little in his chair. 'I don't know. He gave me ten days to think it over. I have a feeling that I may well be jumping out of the frying pan into the fire. Old Curtis has all the signs of being as big a swine as Uncle Daniel and then, in the course of the interview, it became crystal clear where exactly my value to March and Jays lay. Uncle Daniel's got several new processes just about coming to fruition. Mr Curtis was very tactful about it, but I rather gathered that March and Jays weren't terribly interested in me without the processes. Plenty of food for thought there, as they say. And if my uncle Daniel ever finds out he'll flay me alive, to say nothing of what my wife will do. So' — he straightened up with a tired half-smile — 'I should be very grateful for your discretion.'

Dover grunted. 'You can rely on us. I'm sorry you've been put to all this inconvenience but there are some people who can't resist chasing after red herrings.'

MacGregor showed Mr Topping-Wibbley out and then came back, turning the visiting card over and over in his hands. 'It looks as though Topping-Wibbley is in the clear, doesn't it, sir? I'll check with this Mr Curtis tomorrow but I'm pretty certain we've got the truth this time.'

Dover loosened his collar. 'No,' he said.

'No what, sir?'

'Not tomorrow, laddie. Tonight.'

'Eh?'

'Why don't you clean your ears out? I said you'll go and see this Curtis fellow tonight. Do you want me to spell it out for you?'

'Tonight, sir?'

'You started all this, laddie, and you're damned well going to finish it. Teach you a lesson, that will.'

'But, sir, this other firm's nearly sixty miles away! And Mr Curtis won't be there at this time of night and we haven't got his home address.'

'My heart's bleeding for you,' said Dover with massive indifference.

'And I told the chauffeur we wouldn't need the Rolls again tonight,' wailed MacGregor. 'Surely we can leave this till tomorrow, sir?'

'Never put off till tomorrow what you can do today,' said Dover with a smugness that made MacGregor itch to belt him one. 'And the Rolls is out anyhow. Mr Wibbley might find out where you'd been and start putting two and two together. And that wouldn't be fair to poor Mr Topping-Wibbley, would it? I expect there's a bus or a train or something.' He grinned evilly to himself. 'If I was you I'd be getting a move-on. Otherwise you'll be at it all night.'

'Perhaps Mr Topping-Wibbley knows Curtis's home address?' suggested MacGregor hopefully.

'Oh, no!' Dover was quick to scotch this possible easing of the burden. 'Discretion we promised him and discretion he's going to get. No phone calls. His missus might answer or listen in or something. And don't go trying to scrounge a car from the local coppers, either. They're riddled with old Wibbley's spies.'

MacGregor recognized defeat when he saw it but he couldn't resist one last appeal to Dover's non-existent good nature.

Dover cut the protestations short. 'You're wasting time, laddie!'

Speechless with fury MacGregor left, almost slamming the door behind him.

Never much of a one for standing on his dignity, Dover raised himself up on one elbow and blew a resounding raspberry in the wake of his disgruntled sergeant. Then he had a good old chuckle to himself.

In point of fact the man in the green M.G. was a perfectly innocent sales representative from the U-Kleen-It Carpet Sweeper Company. A few days before her death Cynthia had written to ask where she could buy their latest product and had been rewarded by a personal call. The U-Kleen-It Carpet Sweeper Company man wasn't much of a reader and by the time he'd caught up with the details of the murder it was all over bar the shouting. He just thought he wouldn't bother coming forward with his evidence, and Dover never did find out who he was.

Chapter Ten

MACGREGOR only just got back to Pott Winckle in time for the inquest. He had had an adventurous night but Dover meanly refused to listen to anything about it.

'Cut out the sob stuff,' he ordered. 'Has Topping-Wibbley got an alibi or hasn't he?'

'I'm afraid he has, sir.'

'Well, what are you bitching about, then?'

MacGregor sighed. He'd had no dinner, no sleep and no breakfast and was feeling thoroughly fed up. Not that he expected any sympathy from Dover. They sat together, squeezed up on a rather uncomfortable wooden bench, and waited for the inquest on the late Cynthia Perking to begin.

The room in which the inquest was to be held was very small. It had been chosen deliberately. None of the officials upon whom the selection fell had thought for one moment that the inhabitants of Pott Winckle would be so insensitive as to attempt to intrude upon the Wibbley family in their grief, but, as the Town Clerk put it, there was no use handing it to the nosey buggers on a plate. The room, therefore, was not only small, it was also remote. No members of the general public had dared ask where the inquest was to be held and the bolder spirits of the fourth estate had been given, in all bad faith, directions which led them to a Congregational hall at the other end of the town.

The coroner, therefore, conducted his brief inquiry before a very select audience. Only those, like Dover and MacGregor, who were duty-bound to be present and the Wibbley family were crammed into the inadequate benches. None of John Perking's relations had felt it incumbent on them to rally round, but the Wibbleys were there in force, intent presumably not only that justice should be done but that it should be done discreetly.

'Who's that?' whispered Dover, indicating a pugnacious little woman who was making her second entrée. Much to her disgust she had been refused admittance the first time on account of two small hairy dogs lurking one under each armpit.

'I believe that's Daniel Wibbley's wife, sir,' said MacGregor, finding that his insecure perch at one end of the bench was being placed in jeopardy as the estranged Mrs Wibbley rammed herself in at the other end. 'I say, steady on, sir! You'll have me on the floor.'

'It's getting like the Black Hole of Calcutta in here!' gasped Dover, using his elbows to some purpose. 'Shove up, Mac-Gregor, I haven't room to breathe!'

'I can't, sir!' protested MacGregor, and braced himself. 'Let's push together, sir!'

But, before the combined weight of the two Scotland Yard detectives could be brought into effective play, the coroner entered and everybody stood up. Not everybody sat down again in response to the coroner's self-satisfied nod. Dover, a slow mover at the best of times, had paused to catch his breath and the ranks had closed inexorably beneath him.

The coroner stared at him in horror. Everything was supposed to have been so carefully arranged. The last thing anyone wanted was a sensational development. Mr Wibbley would be furious.

'Did you wish to address me, Chief Inspector?' he asked fearfully.

'Eh?' Dover was somewhat disconcerted to find that everybody was staring at him. 'Er – no, no.'

'Oh,' said the coroner.

There was only one thing to do. Dover sat down. Seventeen and a quarter stone, none the less heavy for being mostly fat, landed with a crunch on the knees of Sergeant MacGregor and a young lady who was now sitting next to him. Understandably they pulled away from the crushing burden and Dover's ample buttocks again made contact with the wooden seat. He wriggled himself into a more secure position and an elderly gentleman six places away fell with a crash on to the floor.

'Order, order!' rapped the coroner, glaring in outrage. 'If there are any more of these disgusting disturbances I shall clear the court!' A policeman looked questioningly at him. Feeling very masterful the coroner inclined his head. The policeman bent down and assisted the old gentleman to his feet and then, maintaining a firm hold on the scruff of his neck, proceeded to evict him none too gently from the court.

Having thus asserted the ancient authority of his office the coroner calmly opened his inquest. Six and a half minutes later he closed it, just as calmly and with an air of great satisfaction. Only the barest bones had been uncovered and then the lid had been slapped smartly on, the police having requested and been granted a lengthy adjournment while they completed their inquiries.

All stood respectfully as the coroner, with an obsequious half-nod to Daniel Wibbley, withdrew.

'Thank God for that!' exclaimed Dover, struggling to his feet. 'Let's get the hell out of here!'

MacGregor was right behind him. For some time his sensitive nose had been troubled by a peculiar smell which seemed to be permeating the courtroom. Since the proceedings had been so dull he had spent his time trying to track down the source of this unpleasant odour. It was without much surprise that he finally decided that it must be Dover. Somebody ought to tell the old pig, thought MacGregor resentfully and tried to breathe as little as possible. It really was too much. A Detective Chief Inspector from New Scotland Yard ponging like an overripe midden! So, when Dover indicated that he was all for beating a quick retreat, MacGregor lent a more than willing shoulder.

There seemed to be some sort of a jam up by the door. MacGregor peered over the intervening heads. The maternal and paternal connections of the late Cynthia Perking appeared to be disputing matters of precedence.

'To be trampled on' – Mrs Wibbley's resounding tones effectively stilled the noise in the rest of the room – 'at one's own daughter's inquest! After all I have gone through, this is the last straw!'

Her husband looked down his nose at her. 'If you are comparing yourself with a camel, my dear Rosalind, you will hardly induce me to quarrel with you. And now, since passing through this doorway appears to be a matter of life and death to you, kindly proceed. No doubt one of your disgusting curs is even now rupturing itself with yelping for you. A less forgiving man than myself might be tempted to point out that, had you reared your daughter as devotedly as your rear those filthy animals, we should not be meeting now in such tragic circumstances.'

'You swine!' roared Mrs Wibbley, struggling to free her umbrella arm from the mass of bodies pressing round her. 'You sanctimonious, unmitigated swine! I suppose it's my fault that Cynthia didn't have a mother?'

Her husband's face composed itself into a sneer. 'It is, my dear Rosalind, hardly mine.'

'You drove me out!'

'If you had not behaved like a bitch in the manger and refused to divorce me, as any self-respecting wife would have done, I could have provided my daughter with any one of a hundred mother-substitutes.'

'I have no doubt you would have done,' retorted Mrs Wibbley grimly, 'and Cynthia would have been forced out of her home even earlier, instead of waiting till she was eighteen.'

'My daughter was not forced out of her home!' Mr Wibbley shouted. 'I opposed that disastrous marriage with all my might and main. The girl was wilful, pig-headed and obstinate, and we all know from where she inherited those attributes. Neither they nor a thoughtless lack of consideration for the feelings of others are characteristic of my family.'

'Your family?' began Mrs Wibbley scornfully, but she was interrupted.

'Daniel! Rosalind! This is no place for quarrelling!' It was a woman close behind Mrs Wibbley. She pushed her hat back into position on her head and tried to include both the contestants in a chiding smile. 'I did so hope that Cynthia's death would have brought you two dear unhappy mortals closer together.'

'My God, Ottilia!' Mr Wibbley raised his eyes accusingly to the skies. 'That's all we needed! What do you think this is—a peepshow? I'm only surprised you didn't bring your blasted father with you. Oh, I forgot—they don't provide liquid refreshments at inquests.'

'Papa was here, Daniel,' Ottilia reproached him gently, 'but he—er—had to leave before the inquest actually started. He's no longer a young man, you know, and he was really very upset.'

'I can't think why. To the best of my knowledge he hasn't seen Cynthia since we made the mistake of inviting him to the christening.'

'Well, of course, that just goes to show how little you knew about your daughter, doesn't it, Daniel dear?' Ottilia asked nastily. 'She was a frequent visitor to our house before she married. She and Mildred were very close when they were girls.'

'Mildred? Who the devil's Mildred?'

'Mildred is my daughter, Daniel, as you know perfectly well. Mildred, say good morning to your uncle.'

'I am not her uncle,' snapped Mr Wibbley, 'and if she has the impertinence to address me as such I shall take legal proceedings to restrain her. Our connection, thank God, is only through marriage and, although not remote enough, it can in no circumstances be considered a close relationship.'

'I'm your wife's first cousin!' Ottilia objected.

'But not, thank God, mine! And while we are on the subject, madam, I may as well inform you that I consider your daughter's presence here—to say nothing of your own and your decrepit father's—to be the nadir of bad taste.'

'We came here to support Rosalind. In times like these a family should hang together.'

'Now, there's a happy thought!' leered Mr Wibbley. 'The vision of the Sinclair family all hanging in a row together—from the gallows tree! Because that's where you ought to be—the lot of you! If it hadn't been for your simpering, snivelling brat here none of this would have happened. She's responsible!' He pointed a dramatic and accusing finger at a young woman cowering behind Ottilia and Rosalind.

'He's mad!' wailed Ottilia, turning to enfold the girl in a protective embrace. 'Don't listen to him, my baby! Grief has turned his brain. Oh,'—she twisted round to confront Mr Wibbley again—'if my dear husband were alive, he would deal with you, you fiend! He wouldn't allow you to speak to us like this.'

'For the price of a packet of cigarettes your late and unlamented husband would have jumped through a hoop backwards. Apart from your father he was the biggest sponger it has ever been my misfortune to encounter. An attribute, I may add, which has been passed on undiminished to your daughter, Mildred. I warned Cynthia time and time again that Mildred was just out for what she could get—old dresses, broken bits of jewellery, half-used pots of face cream. She'd take anything.'

'But not, I fancy,' said Ottilia, drawing herself up with great dignity, 'men.'

Mr Wibbley's face blackened with rage. 'And what is that disgusting remark supposed to mean?'

'I fancy you know perfectly well, Daniel. We Sinclairs may be poor but we have our standards. It's all a matter of breeding, but one can hardly expect a man who trades in water closets to understand that.'

Mr Wibbley turned in a fury to his wife. 'Rosalind, you'd better get your foul-mouthed cousin out of here before I do something I may be sorry for!'

'Oh no, Daniel,'—Ottilia stood her ground—'not until I've had my say. Cynthia *stole* John Perking from Mildred in a most despicable way. They were practically engaged, poor children, until your daughter came along and broke the whole thing up. As you have been so coarse as to mention, Mildred has nothing, but your precious daughter had to steal from her the one thing she had got. I shall never forgive Cynthia for that, never. Mildred understood John. She could have helped him. They would have made a happy and successful couple. Cynthia destroyed all hopes of that, spitefully and selfishly.'

Mr Wibbley looked astounded. 'You are complaining because your daughter didn't marry a murderer?' he howled.

Ottilia got her last thrust in. 'John would not have been a murderer', she said, 'if Mildred had been his wife.'

'She's got a point there, sir,' said MacGregor as he pocketed his change. 'It takes two to make a murder: the killer and his victim.'

Dover poured the best part of a pint of bitter straight down his throat. 'Phew, that's better!' He belched loudly and finished off the rest of the beer. 'Well, since you twist my arm, laddie, I'll have the same again.'

They were sitting in the saloon bar of the nearest public house. Dover had headed for it, like a pigeon returning to its loft, as soon as they had extricated themselves from the court room.

The various members of the Wibbley and Sinclair families had continued washing their dirty linen for a considerable time and with much gusto. Grudges which had been rankling for years were dragged out and polished up. The Wibbleys, accused of being jumped-up artisans, retaliated by branding the Sinclairs as impoverished snobs. The ridiculous clothes worn by old Mrs Wibbley at her son's wedding twenty-odd years ago were neutralized by the disgusting behaviour of Sir Quintin Sinclair on the same happy occasion. In the joy of battle none of the participants gave much thought to the grievous and tragic circumstances which had brought them together. At long last, however, both sides ran out of effective ammunition and they parted. The Wibbleys swept off in an impressive array of Rolls-Royces and Bentleys and foreign sports cars while the entire Sinclair representation piled, together with six smelly Yorkshire terriers, into one battered Morris Minor.

'Get us a packet of crisps while you're about it,' said Dover as MacGregor slid over the second pint of beer. 'I dunno,' he went on, 'I reckon Perking is a bad 'un through and through. Born to hang. Got what you might call a predilection for murder. Look what he did to me!' Dover examined his face in the mirror behind the bar. 'Came at me like a ruddy maniac, he did. Eyes staring, foaming at the mouth. I know he only looks a little tich of a chap, but they've got the strength of ten when they go berserk like that.'

'You think he's insane then, sir?'

Dover choked on his beer. 'No, I damned well don't!' he spluttered. 'He's as compos mentis as I am. And don't let me catch you spreading it around that he's potty. That'd put the blooming kibosh on everything.'

'I really don't see why, sir.' MacGregor, in a seemingly casual manner, edged his stool two or three inches away from Dover's. There was no doubt about it. The Chief Inspector had got B.O. in a big way. 'I can't see that it makes much difference.'

'You wouldn't,' groused Dover and shuffled his stool closer to MacGregor. It was difficult to know quite how to express what he wanted to say. Had MacGregor been a more sympathetic, broad-minded character one could have spoken frankly to him. But the truth of the matter was that MacGregor was a sanctimonious, straight-laced young prig and wouldn't for one moment understand the special relationship which existed between Dover and Mr Wibbley. How could Dover reveal to this unwordly idealist that Dover's future well-being depended on John Perking being kept in prison for the rest of his life. Dover knew the Mr Wibbleys of this world only too well: no stinging condemnation by the trial judge meant no affluent sinecure for the ex-Detective Chief Inspector: no public outcry at Perking's heinous crime and Dover could sweat it out in Scotland Yard until he retired.

And sweat it out was right, too. It wouldn't have been so bad, Dover thought disconsolately, if he could just sit on his backside and take it easy, but there were too many people gunning for him. The Assistant Commissioner himself, to name but one. At his last meeting for his senior officers he was reliably reported as blaming the entire rise in the rates of undetected crime on the continued presence of Dover on the police payroll. And it was an open secret that there was an O.B.E. waiting for the man who got rid of him. Dover had few illusions about the security of his tenure. It was all jealousy, of course, but that didn't mean he hadn't got to watch his step. He couldn't even trust his sergeant, he thought bitterly, as he watched that young man waiting with resignation for him to continue the conversation.

'Well, it does,' said Dover.

'Does what, sir?'

'Make a difference, you damned fool!' Dover gazed into the depths of his tankard. 'I don't know quite how I can put this to you, MacGregor, but for a chap like me this business of solving crimes and bringing the villain to book is sort of like a crusade.'

MacGregor's eyebrows rose.

'Yes,' said Dover, rather satisfied with his comparison, 'like a crusade. Being a copper isn't just a job for me – it's what you might call a mission. I feel I'm here to make this country a decent place to live in. To the best of my poor ability,' he added modestly. 'So, you see, getting a lousy little burk like Perking convicted really *matters* to me.'

'Well, it matters to me, too, sir,' said MacGregor, drawing his head away as far as he could. 'After all, it's a question of professional pride, isn't it?'

Dover produced a sad smile. 'Ah, pride!' He shook his head in gentle reproof. 'No, whatever anybody might say about me, I don't think they could accuse me of being proud. No, I think my attitude to criminals is a more humble one than yours, laddie. More Christian, really.'

'Christian, sir?'

'Yes,' said Dover truculently, beginning to wonder why on earth he'd ever started this. 'I want to see 'em suffer.' He heard the sharp intake of MacGregor's breath. 'Well, and what's wrong with that, eh? They've done wrong—haven't they?—and they've damned well got to pay for it. I can't see anything wrong with that. I suppose you're one of these blasted namby-pamby interfering bastards who'd just give 'em a pat on the head and say you naughty boy don't do it again? Make me sick, your sort do! No flogging, no hanging and bedside lamps all round! You want your fat heads examining! It was a bad day for Old England when you nits got hanging stopped. All right, so murdering louts like John Perking can't swing for it these days. Well, I happen to consider it my bounden duty to see that he pays for it as far as he can. And that doesn't mean lolling around in comfort in a criminal lunatic asylum.'

MacGregor was feeling a trifle confused. What was he bumbling on about now? 'Well, I can understand somebody like Mr Wibbley feeling that way, sir, but ... '

'Let me tell you', snarled Dover, thrusting his face into MacGregor's, 'that I couldn't feel more strongly if Cynthia Perking had been my own daughter. John Perking was a callous, cold-blooded and deliberate murderer and it's our duty to demonstrate that to the court that convicts and sentences him—get it?'

MacGregor was far from getting it but he dutifully nodded his head. When Dover was in this sort of mood the only safe course was to humour him. Or, if possible, change the conversation. 'Will you be wanting me for anything special after lunch, sir?'

Dover was instantly suspicious. 'Why?'

'Well, to tell you the truth, sir, I'm feeling pretty whacked. I didn't get to bed at all last night, sir, and ... '

'Marvellous, isn't it?' Dover addressed his question to two elderly crones guzzling neat gin at the other end of the bar. They exchanged knowing glances and sniggered. 'As soon as you're asked to do a bit of work, you crack up. I don't know how you've got the nerve to ask, honestly I don't. If I'd said that to my chief inspector when I was a sergeant, he'd have blasted me from here to Halifax. And I'd have deserved it, too. What are you proposing, laddie? That I go slogging on while you have a quiet kip and catch up on your beauty sleep?'

'Of course not, sir. If there's work to be done, I shall be only too willing to do it. It's just that I thought … '

'Well, there is some work to be done,' said Dover quickly. 'As it happens.'

'Very well, sir,' said MacGregor stiffly.

There was a pause.

'Those pies look nice,' said Dover with a certain wistfulness.

MacGregor glanced at the clock. 'Won't it spoil your lunch, sir?'

Dover shook his head and moved the mustard pot nearer to hand. 'Eat little and often, that's what the doctor told me.'

MacGregor ordered a pie. 'What was it you wanted me to do this afternoon, sir?'

'Eh?' Dover chewed resentfully on a tough piece of gristle. Trust MacGregor to go and ruin what few pleasures he got these days. No wonder his stomach was in the state it was in when people kept upsetting him every time he took a mouthful of food. The gristle defeated Dover's dentures and he spat it out on his plate. MacGregor pointedly looked the other way. 'You'd better check up on that dark-green car, hadn't you?' said Dover with sudden inspiration.

'Dark-green car, sir?'

'Naturally.' Dover took another mouthful of pie and spoke through it. 'Somebody called to see Cynthia Perking that afternoon, didn't they? All you've proved so far is that it wasn't Topping-Wibbley. Well, that's not good enough, is it, laddie?'

'But, sir, I don't see how we can get any further. We haven't anything but the barest description to go … '

'You'd better go round that housing estate again,' said Dover ruthlessly. 'Have another chat with those women in

Birdsfoot-Trefoil Close. You never know, maybe they've remembered something they forgot to tell you the first time you asked 'em.'

'I doubt it, sir. Of course, sir,' — MacGregor shot a sly look at Dover — 'I'm probably approaching it in quite the wrong manner. I expect if somebody with your skill and experience was to go round and question ... '

Dover rose up from his bar stool and began buttoning up his overcoat. 'Just watch it, laddie,' he warned. 'Don't go pushing your luck.'

Chapter Eleven

'Sex,' said Dover with the air of one who has made a significant discovery.

The scene was the pre-breakfast get-together in Dover's bedroom. The Chief Inspector liked to refer to it as his early-morning conference but this was a trifle grandiose for a meeting which came about only because Dover didn't like going down to breakfast by himself. As usual he wasn't ready when MacGregor's tap was heard. MacGregor poked his head round the door.

'Oh, I'm sorry, sir. I thought I heard you say come in.'

'You did,' said Dover. 'Well, come on! And get that door closed. It's like a howling gale blowing through here.'

MacGregor sidled unwillingly into the room and scurried, eyes averted, over to the window. 'It's still raining, sir,' he remarked in a voice that was not perfectly steady.

'Hm,' said Dover without much interest. He continued to contemplate his reflection in the full-length mirror. He was wearing nothing but a rather yellowed, rather shrunken, long-sleeved woollen vest. 'Sex,' he said again and reached for his matching underpants.

'Sir?' said MacGregor, not caring to turn round.

'Sex,' repeated Dover with a grunt as he tugged his pants up over his paunch. 'Where are my socks? Yes, sex. John Perking's motive. If it wasn't money it must be sex, mustn't it?'

'Well, sir,' began MacGregor doubtfully.

'We've established', Dover continued, picking up a shirt that MacGregor would have been ashamed to deposit in a dustbin, 'that Cynthia Perking wasn't indulging in a bit of the old hanky-panky—so where does that leave us?'

'But everybody says the same about Perking himself, sir. His sister, the neighbours—all the evidence we've had. They all say that Perking was devoted to his wife. There hasn't been the slightest hint from anyone that he was unfaithful to her in any way.'

Dover picked up his tie and looked at it without pleasure. It was his wife's invention. The knot and the part of the tie that hangs down the front of the shirt were quite normal, but, instead of the piece that goes round the neck under the collar, there was a broad strip of black elastic. Oh well, thought Dover as he pulled the elastic over his head, I suppose it saves a bit of trouble.

MacGregor, who had turned round at this critical moment, shuddered.

'You know what I think?' asked Dover, ignorant of the shock he had given his sergeant's sartorial susceptibilities. 'I reckon Perking has got himself a juicy little popsie shacked up somewhere on the quiet.'

'But, sir, absolutely everybody agrees … '

'I don't give a damn about what everybody agrees,' retorted Dover. 'If he has got himself a bit of homework he's not going to advertise it in the local paper, is he? Of course he'd keep it quiet. The way I see it, he marries Cynthia for her money but, what with one thing and another, he can't get his hands on the lolly. Meanwhile he's under pressure from this other popsie. It's me you love, she keeps on yacking at him, so why don't you make an honest woman of me? Have a bit of patience, he says, and once I get the money we can both of us live a life of luxury. But, after three years of waiting they get a bit cheesed off with it so Perking does his wife in so that he can nip off with his girl friend. It's only guesswork so far,' he admitted with touching modesty, 'but I reckon it hangs together pretty well.'

'Well, as a theory, sir, I suppose it has got its points but, if you don't mind my saying so, sir, it isn't exactly watertight, is it?'

'Isn't it?' Dover pouted. He didn't take kindly to criticism, especially when it came from sergeants.

'Well, sir, apart from the fact that there hasn't been the faintest whisper that Perking was engaging in extra-marital activities, why on earth should he kill his wife just when he was on the verge of success?'

'Huh?'

'The pregnancy, sir. Why kill her the minute he hears that she's pregnant? Everybody agrees that with a grandchild on the way Daniel Wibbley would have given in. He told you so himself, didn't he? According to your theory, sir, Perking upped and killed the golden goose before she'd even had chance to lay him a golden egg.'

'We don't know for sure that she'd phoned him and told him about the baby,' Dover pointed out.

'I'm sure a few inquiries can clear up that point, sir.'

'And', continued Dover, determined not to be out-argued by logic or reason, 'for all we know it may have been the fact that he found out his wife was expecting that shoved him over the edge.'

'Sir?'

'Where are my boots?' grumbled Dover. 'Oh? Well, push 'em over, laddie. And you might as well help me on with 'em while you're at it. I think that rotten little bastard Perking damaged my back. I've got a funny sort of pain that shoots from here to here.' Dover twisted himself round awkwardly and vaguely indicated a couple of unlikely spots on his back. 'Excruciating, it is, at times. I sometimes wonder how I carry on, I do really. It's just sheer courage and devotion to duty that keeps me going, you know. Most men would have taken to their beds if they'd gone through half what I've had to put up with. That's my trouble – I never give a thought to myself. Here, not too tight with those laces! I shouldn't have given up that bathchair thing as soon as I did,' he added moodily. 'I suppose you sent it back, did you?'

'Yes, sir.' MacGregor's answer was firm. 'They were very grateful. They said they had another patient waiting for it. You were saying, sir, that Perking may have killed his wife *because* she was pregnant.'

'Eh? Oh, yes—well, look at the timing. As soon as he hears she's in the family way he beats her head in. Course, it might just be a coincidence. Here, help me on with my coat. But suppose Perking has got fed up with waiting for the money and decides the girl friend is a better bet than the missus? He's all set to pack his marriage in and get annulment or whatever it is because she can't have kids when, out of the blue, he discovers she's pregnant. Now he can't get away so easily so— he kills her.'

MacGregor held Dover's jacket for him and wondered if he could wash his hands before he went down to breakfast. The garment really had a most creepy-crawly feel about it. He considered Dover's argument doubtfully. 'It doesn't sound very likely, does it, sir? There are plenty of ways of shedding a wife these days without killing her.'

'Yes, but if she was barren Perking could have divorced her, couldn't he? If not, she'd have had to divorce him with the girl friend as co-respondent. Well, look at her mother. She wouldn't divorce Daniel Wibbley, would she? Maybe the daughter's a chip off the old block.'

'Yes,' said MacGregor, still unconvinced.

'Murder's been done for less, laddie.'

'What about Daniel Wibbley himself, sir? Suppose he made another attempt to buy Perking off only, this time, Perking agrees. He'll get the marriage annulled in return for a really colossal pay-off. He's all set when Cynthia phones up and says she's going to have a baby. That means he can't get his free-dom or collect the bribe, so he kills her.'

'Same difference, isn't it, laddie? Motive's money or sex or both. I still think that the fact the wife was pregnant has got something to do with it.'

'Perhaps Perking just doesn't like children, sir?'

Dover frowned. 'There's no need to be flippant, laddie! Anyhow, we'll have to get down to it.'

'Down to what, sir?'

'A full examination of Perking, of course. In depth.'

'You're not going to interview him again, sir, are you?'

'Not bleeding likely!' snorted Dover with some energy. 'No, we'll poke around a bit in his background. In a small town like this we ought to be able to dig up some dirt.'

The first spadeful was turned over in the Safari-Agogo Travel Agency.

It was a very modest establishment. In the absence of John Perking it was being manned solely by his assistant manager, Miss Dorothea Bloxwich.

'There's just the two of us, usually,' she explained as she pushed her knitting out of sight under the counter. 'When we're busy we take on a temporary but that's only in the early summer, really. I suppose you want to see round his office?'

' 'Sright,' said Dover gazing placidly at a life-size cardboard cut-out of a Hawaiian lovely.

Miss Bloxwich raised the counter flap. 'Through here,' she said. 'Not that it's a proper office, more a sort of a storeroom, really. Still, he always sat in here. Thought it gave the branch a bit of tone, you know, him lording it in his private office and me stuck out in the shop part like a lemon. Made me laugh it did, really.' She tossed an inordinate quantity of streaky blonde hair and fluttered heavily mascaraed eyes at MacGregor. 'I was wondering when the cops'd be coming round. From London, aren't you? I'm hoping to get transferred to London myself.'

'That'll be nice,' said MacGregor politely.

'Better than this dump,' agreed Miss Bloxwich, wriggling the chewing gum from one side of her mouth to the other. 'Like a morgue it is here, really. The Safari-Agogo's quite a big organization, you know. S'got hundreds of branches all over the place. The Head Office is in London, of course. In Bond Street. That's in the West End, you know.'

'Is that where you hope to be working?' asked MacGregor.

'It'd do for a start,' the young lady observed casually. 'I thought they'd have been saying something before now. I mean, I told them right away what had happened as soon as they arrested Mr Perking. I thought they'd have offered me a move then, but they just told me to carry on as best I could for a few days. But you can't expect me to stay on here, can you? I mean, working with a murderer – it's not nice, is it? If you ask me the least they can do is offer me a transfer to London, don't you think?'

'How long have you been working here?' Dover had sat himself down at the desk and was desultorily opening and shutting the drawers.

'Oh, ever since I left school. Six months. I went to the Grammar, you know. I've got two "O" levels. Safari-Agogo won't take you if you haven't had a good education.' She examined herself with obvious appreciation in a mirror hanging on the wall. 'That's why I want to get to London. I'm wasted down here.'

'You'd know John Perking pretty well, then,' said Dover. 'What did you think of him?'

'Bit of a stick-in-the-mud, if you ask me,' replied Miss Bloxwich, rearranging her hair so that it covered one eye in a most seductive manner. 'Married, too. I don't go much on married men, myself.' She eyed MacGregor. 'I'll bet you're not married, are you?'

'No,' said MacGregor, feeling rather uncomfortable.

'Thought not. You're just about the right age, too. I prefer mature men, myself.'

'What about Perking?' said Dover.

'What about him?'

'Did he ever try getting fresh with you?'

'Him?' Miss Bloxwich shrieked with laughter. 'I should like to have seen him try! Why, I could eat two of him before breakfast and never notice.'

Dover slumped back in his chair and regarded Miss Bloxwich with intense dislike. Trust a woman! At first glance she had looked an ideal proposition – a tasty bit of fluff with which John Perking could have whiled away his business hours. It would have all fitted in so nicely – had the principals been halfway accommodating. No need for furtive meetings or veiled communications which Pott Winckle's voluntary cheka would have blown sky high in a couple of minutes. Just a nice snug little love-nest tucked away at the back of the Safari-Agogo Travel Agency to which the pair of them could repair with the greatest of ease.

That's the trouble with police work these days, Dover ruminated crossly as he watched Miss Bloxwich displaying a stretch of shapely thigh for MacGregor's delectation, no bloody co-operation from the public. John Perking must have been a right old damp squib and no mistake. Surely any man with a drop of red blood in his veins would have availed himself of this eager and willing opportunity?

'Staying long in Pott?' asked Miss Bloxwich idly.

'Well, I don't really know,' MacGregor answered feebly. 'It all depends.'

'Thought you might like to buy us a coke one evening,' said Miss Bloxwich with a cheeky smile. 'I finish here at half past five and I often go to the coffee bar up the street. They've got a groovy juke box there.'

'Well,' said MacGregor, gazing at Dover for help, 'that sounds very nice.'

'You'll come then?' Miss Bloxwich knew what happened to girls who didn't strike when the iron was lukewarm.

Dover sighed. He was beginning to lose interest in this blessed case, and that was the truth of it. Still, he sighed again, he supposed he'd just have to soldier on. He thought of the job as Chief Security Officer at Wibbley Ware in an attempt to cheer himself up. Four thousand a year sounded all right, but if you had to kill yourself earning it … He wondered if Daniel Wibbley was likely to be an indulgent employer. Probably not.

MacGregor was still sending out distress signals.

Dover made an effort to pull himself together. 'Who did your job before you came here?'

Miss Bloxwich gave a little start. She'd forgotten that the weird old grandpa model was still there. 'Oh, a girl called Elsie Long. She'd been here since the year dot. Got into a rut, if you ask me. She was here even before Mr Perking came.

They had a bigger staff then, you see. Then, when Mr Perking married Daniel Wibbley's daughter, they moved the manager to another branch and gave him the job. Elsie Long was ever so bitter about it. Well, she'd forgotten more about this lark than John Perking'd know if he tried from now till the cows come home. She thought she ought to have been made manager, you see. She'd been here much longer than Perking had.'

'But he got the job?'

'Well, natch! He was Daniel Wibbley's son-in-law, wasn't he?' She grinned. 'Elsie Long made him pay for it, though. She could be a real devil when she put her mind to it.'

'Where is she now?'

'I dunno. Somewhere in Australia or somewhere.'

'Australia?'

'Her husband emigrated. That's why she packed it in here.'

Bang went number two. Dover lost heart. He flapped his hand at MacGregor as an indication that the burden of interrogation had now been chucked into his lap.

'Well now,' said MacGregor briskly, 'the day Mrs Perking was murdered – did you notice anything unusual about Mr Perking's behaviour?'

Miss Bloxwich shook her head. 'Not specially. He'd been ever so touchy for a week or so, actually. You never knew where you were with him. I told my dad, much more of this, I said, and I'll jack it in. I'm getting pretty cheesed off with it here anyhow.'

'Could you be a bit more precise?' asked MacGregor. 'What do you mean – touchy?'

'Oh, I dunno. Touchy. You know, like he was all tense and sort of worried about something.'

'And this was only in the last week or two?'

'Well, he hasn't ever been what you might call a little ray of sunshine, but he had got worse lately. Always niggling, you know. I said, for God's sake, I said, we don't get anybody coming in once in a blue moon – what difference does a few minutes make? He used to sit at that desk with his blooming watch in his hand ... ' She shrugged her shoulders.

'And you've no idea what was worrying him?'

'Not the faintest. It was all the same to me. I only work here, you know.'

'Did he used to have any visitors?'

'Here? I dunno. Sometimes he used to see some of the customers if there was something difficult they wanted. That wasn't often. If they just wanted leaflets or to book on a tour I used to deal with them. It's dead easy, you know.'

'What about during your lunch hour?' asked MacGregor shrewdly. He might have made quite a good detective if fate hadn't entwined his destiny with Dover's. 'Mr Perking brought sandwiches, didn't he? What about you? Did you have your lunch here in the office?'

'Sometimes,' admitted Miss Bloxwich exploring a cavity in her back teeth with the aid of a silvered fingernail. 'Sometimes I'd go along to the caff and have a coke and a bun. It all depended.'

'On what?'

Miss Bloxwich looked vacant. 'I dunno.'

'Could Mr Perking have been entertaining a friend – a lady, say – here in this office while you were out at lunch?'

Miss Bloxwich's mouth gaped open. Then she let out an uninhibited shriek of mirth. 'Don't be filthy!' she giggled. 'Stuck up old Perking and a lady friend? In here? Course not! You cops haven't half got sexy minds, haven't you? Old Perking wouldn't have the guts for one thing, and for another I'd have spotted something for sure. I'm not a kid, you know. Besides, he wasn't a bit like that. I've been here six months and he's never made a pass at me. And you can't say I'm not attractive to men, can you?' She fluttered her eyelids provocatively at MacGregor.

'It all depends on the men,' rumbled Dover nastily from his seat at the desk. 'Let's get back to Perking. Did he sit in this morgue all day or did he ever go out for a bit?'

Miss Bloxwich pulled a mocking face at MacGregor. 'Oh, charming, I'm sure!' She tossed an answer over her shoulder to Dover. 'Course he went out sometimes. We both did. Not every day we didn't but, whenever we needed to, we went. What else? Matter of fact, he went out that morning.'

'What morning?'

'The morning of the day he killed her, of course,' said Miss Bloxwich impatiently. 'Jesus, that's what we're talking about, isn't it?'

'Here, just you watch your language!' Dover warned her. 'Beats me where you bleeding kids pick it all up from. Now, let's get on with it! Just tell us as briefly as you can what Perking did that morning.'

Miss Bloxwich was not abashed. 'What morning?' she asked saucily.

Dover ground his teeth in fury.

'Now, come along,' said MacGregor quickly, 'tell us what happened.'

'Well, nothing happened.' Miss Bloxwich was getting bored. 'He got here at five to nine and I came along just afterwards. He's got to get here first, see, because he's got the keys. Well, he came in here and opened the letters and things and I pottered around out there. Then he came out and started griping about the window display and saying it was time we changed it. We'd got a whole lot of stuff about luxury cruises to the West Indies and he said he wanted that stuck in the window. I said who in Pott Winckle was going on a cruise in the middle of winter and he got right shirty about it. Told me off good and proper, he did. Well, it was no skin off my nose. If I did the blasted window I couldn't be doing anything else, could I? Well, he kept popping out and wanting this changed and wanting that changed and criticizing until I was just on the point of telling him what he could do with his bloody posters when he came out with his hat and coat on and said he was going out. And good riddance to bad rubbish, I thought.'

'What time was this?'

'I dunno. Half past ten, quarter to eleven—something like that.'

MacGregor leaned forward. 'Did he tell you where he was going?'

Miss Bloxwich shook her head and concentrated on twisting one strand of hair round and round her finger.

MacGregor was determined to let no stone remain unturned. 'Do you know where he went?'

Miss Bloxwich gazed at him with round blue eyes. And again shook her head.

She looks, thought MacGregor unkindly, like a Guernsey heifer with a low I.Q. 'What time did Perking get back?'

' 'Bout twelve o'clock, maybe.' Miss Bloxwich glanced at him from under light-green eyelids. Quite obviously she had more to tell but she was playing hard to get.

'And?' prompted MacGregor.

'Well,' – Miss Bloxwich licked her lips with relish – 'he looked terrible, he really did. His eyes were staring right out of his head and his face was ashen and his hands were trembling so much that he could hardly get the door open. I've never seen anybody look so terrible. Good heavens, Mr Perking, I said, what on earth's the matter? But he didn't seem to hear me. He staggered past me as though I wasn't there and his breath was coming in great deep gusts and there was a trickle of saliva running … '

' 'Strewth!' said Dover. 'You ought to be writing novels, you ought. Cut out the fancy stuff and get on with it.'

'Well,' – Miss Bloxwich looked offended – 'he was upset about something, so *there*! He just came straight in here and shut the door and he didn't come out again all afternoon.'

Dover sniffed and gazed round the office. 'Where's the telephone?'

'Oh, it's on the counter.'

'Didn't Perking get a phone call when he got back?'

Miss Bloxwich frowned. 'That's right,' she said slowly, 'he did. It was his wife. I'd forgotten about that.'

'Did you hear what she said?'

'No. He just said yes and no and that's nice and then he put the phone down and came back in here and shut himself up again.'

'And you're sure you don't know where he went that morning?' asked MacGregor.

'Quite sure.' Miss Bloxwich was firm.

'Who', asked Dover, 'or what is Nayland?'

'Search me,' said Miss Bloxwich, getting out her powder and lipstick. 'Never heard of it.'

'Nayland, sir?' MacGregor looked across at Dover in some surprise.

'Trouble with you, laddie,' observed Dover as he rose ponderously to his feet, 'is that you're so blooming clever you can't see what's under your nose. Perking's desk diary, see? An appointment on the day he killed his wife, see? It says Nayland, eleven o'clock.'

MacGregor was very annoyed. He didn't like Dover coming up with the answers almost before he – MacGregor – had got round to asking the questions. Of course, any fool sitting there with the diary open in front of him would have seen the relevant entry but MacGregor would have preferred to have made the discovery himself.

'Well,' he said, trying to take it like a good loser, 'Nayland – that's not a very common sort of name, is it, sir? We should be able to track that down fairly easily. I wonder if there's anything in the desk amongst Perking's papers that might give us a clue?'

'I wonder,' said Dover with blistering sarcasm. 'Perhaps you'd care to have a look?'

MacGregor leapt eagerly for the desk, firing questions at Miss Bloxwich about where Mr Perking kept his records and had he got an address book and was she sure she'd never heard the name Nayland before.

Dover lumbered indifferently out of the back office and installed himself on a chair behind the shop counter. Unhurriedly he selected a book from amongst an untidy pile on the shelf and, solemnly licking his thumb, commenced turning over the pages.

When MacGregor at last emerged he found Dover, hands folded across his stomach and eyes closed, still behind the counter. He reached for the telephone.

'Wadderyedoin?' asked Dover, not bothering to open his eyes.

'There's not a mention of Nayland amongst Perking's papers, sir,' explained MacGregor, wondering how much time he wasted spelling out the obvious to his Chief Inspector, 'so I thought I'd ring the local police and see if they'd got any ideas.'

'You never learn, do you, laddie?' murmured Dover in a pitying voice.

'Sir?'

'There's only one Nayland in Pott Winckle.' said Dover with an enormous yawn.

'Only one Nayland, sir?'

'That's right, laddie.'

'But — how do you know that, sir?'

Dover opened his eyes and glared bleakly at his sergeant. 'Because I looked in the telephone directory, you bloody fool.'

'Oh, charming!' said Miss Bloxwich from the open doorway, and giggled.

Chapter Twelve

MacGregor would have been less than human if he hadn't hoped, quite hard, that the Nayland Dover had found in the phone book was not the Nayland they were looking for. Indeed, he felt obliged to point out to Dover, respectfully of course, that Pott Winckle might be swarming with people called Nayland who, for one reason or another, were not telephone subscribers.

'Doubt it,' said Dover comfortably.

'Well, this man certainly isn't Perking's regular doctor, sir. I can assure you of that.'

'Thanks very much,' said Dover.

'Perking had got the name of his own doctor and the name of Miss Bloxwich's doctor written down quite clearly inside the first-aid box, sir.'

'Bully for him,' said Dover.

MacGregor bit his lips and stared out of the car window. They were getting back to the Canal Bank Street end of the town. MacGregor's hopes rose slightly. This was the world that John Perking had tried so hard to escape from. Surely he would have avoided any contact with these humble surroundings if he possibly could?

'Of course, sir, this Nayland Perking went to see, he could just be an ordinary client of some sort. It may have nothing at all to do with our inquiries.'

'True,' agreed Dover with an infuriating reasonableness.

'Miss Bloxwich was not the most reliable of witnesses, sir. She was inclined to dramatize a bit, don't you think? I mean, Perking probably behaved in a perfectly normal manner when he returned to the travel agency.'

'Probably,' said Dover with a smirk.

Dr Nayland didn't even have a brass plate to his name. His surgery had once been a shop. The window had been painted over in a streaky opaque white paint except for a narrowish strip along the top. On the white paint, in gold letters, were displayed Dr Nayland's particulars: Dr J. J. J. Nayland, M.D., B.S., L.R.C.P., M.C. Hours of Consultation: By appointment.

Dover read the notice slowly. The gold paint was in an advanced stage of decay and Dover's eyesight wasn't as sharp as it had been.

'Mm,' he said at last.

'Perhaps we should have phoned first, sir?' said MacGregor, standing on tip-toe in an effort to look over the white paint.

'Hm,' said Dover. 'Well, don't lounge around all day – see if the door's open!'

It was. The old shop bell was still functioning and gave a loud ping as MacGregor, with Dover hot on his heels, stepped across the threshold.

They found themselves in a dimly-lit room, crammed with enormous benches which were evidently the former property of the old London & North-Eastern Railway. The walls were decorated with a proliferation of framed diplomas and photographs. Dover ambled over to have a look at some of them. A little to his surprise he discovered many faces that he knew: General de Gaulle, the late President Kennedy, Haile Selassie, all the four Beatles, Sir Laurence Olivier, Maria Callas and a goodly quota of members of the Royal Family. All, according to the inscriptions, were fulsomely indebted to J. J. J. Nayland for his superb care and medical attention and all had remarkably similar handwriting.

The door leading to the back of the shop opened and a man stood there, looking at his visitors.

'Aha! Good morning, good morning, good morning!' The newcomer moved forward a few steps. 'Oh,' he said in a very wary voice.

'Dr Nayland?' asked MacGregor crisply.

The man hesitated. 'Yes,' he admitted. He came further

into the room, thrusting his hands deep into the pockets of his off-white coat and swaying slightly in his suede boots. His face was adorned with an enormous Battle of Britain moustache and round his neck was, as MacGregor alone noticed, a Brigade of Guards tie. 'What can I do for you chaps?'

'As if you didn't know,' said Dover disagreeably.

Dr Nayland sagged a little. Even his moustache drooped. 'I say,' he said, 'steady on, old man. A chap's innocent until he's proved guilty, isn't he?'

Dover sat himself down on the nearest waiting-room bench. 'Let's be having it,' he rumbled.

'Having what?' Dr Nayland glared indignantly. 'You dicks never change the record, do you? Let's hear the charge first and then I'll see whether I'm going to make a statement or not.'

'Ho, ho!' sneered Dover. 'We shall have to watch our step, MacGregor. We've got one of the old hands here.'

'What's past is past,' snapped Dr Nayland pettishly. 'I'm reinstated now. You blighters never give a chap a chance, do you? I notice you never go pounding up and down Harley Street in your great big boots. Oh no, not you lot! But you'll try and lean on me for doing the same blooming thing, won't you? Just because my patients aren't wealthy society ladies or young gentlemen with uncles in the House of Lords! Makes me sick, it really does! Well, come on—what's the bloody charge?'

'No charge,' said Dover, revealing his dentures in a grin. 'We're just making inquiries, that's all.'

'Oh?' Dr Nayland tossed his head. 'Well, we all know what *that* means, don't we? No bloody evidence, eh? Nothing that'll stand up in a court of law, eh? Well, I can't say I'm surprised. She's mentally deficient that girl, you know, and a lousy little trouble-maker into the bargain. Nobody in their right senses'd believe a word that little tart says. And she's got a record as long as your arm—did you know that?'

'No,' said Dover with remarkable good humour, 'I didn't.'

'Well, she has.' Dr Nayland nodded his head vigorously.

'And so's that brother of hers. I suppose he's in it, too? Well, wherever he got 'em from he didn't get 'em from me. Good grief, I'm an ex-officer of the Royal Army Medical Corps—do you think I don't know how to look after my drugs? Thousands of pounds' worth I had under my care during the war and never a single audit query.'

'Do you know a man called John Perking?' Dover asked suddenly.

Dr Nayland blinked, screwed his face up in thought and then shook his head.

'He's a patient of yours,' Dover asserted with authority.

'A patient?' Dr Nayland thrust his hands even deeper into his pockets. 'Oh well, in that case you'd hardly expect me to remember his name, would you, old man? So many of 'em, you see.' He waved one hand vaguely round the empty waiting room. 'Can't keep tabs on 'em all.'

'Doesn't the name John Perking mean anything to you?' MacGregor asked.

'No. Should it?'

'He's Daniel Wibbley's son-in-law.'

'Oh, yes?'

'It's been in all the papers,' said MacGregor severely.

'Never read 'em, old man. Got enough to do keeping up with all the medical bumph we poor old saw-bones have to read these days.'

'John Perking has been arrested for murdering his wife.'

'Blimey!' Wide eyes stared at MacGregor over the bushy moustache. Dr Nayland looked hopefully at the door leading out to the street and apparently decided that he'd never make it. He turned towards his surgery. 'Hang on a minute, old chap, there's something I've just got to see to.'

'Leave the door open,' advised Dover.

'What? Oh, yes. Naturally.'

Dr Nayland disappeared into his surgery. There was the sound of a filing cabinet being opened, the clink of a glass and the soft gurgle of liquid being poured out of a bottle. Dr Nayland came back. There was slightly more colour in his face and he was dabbing his moustache with a huge gaudy silk handkerchief. 'That's better,' he observed, carefully not looking at anybody. 'Purely medicinal, of course. Got to watch the old ticker, eh? Legacy of the war, I'm afraid.'

'John Perking,' Dover reminded him.

'Yes – well – you can't hold me responsible, can you? I mean, if a doctor prescribes a certain treatment for one of his patients, he does it in good faith, doesn't he? It's not his fault if the patient tries the stuff out on the cat or whatever, is it?'

'Perking beat his wife's head in with a poker,' said Dover impatiently.

Dr Nayland looked happier. 'Did he, by gum? Sounds a violent-tempered fellow.'

'He is,' said Dover, with feeling.

'But, what's it got to do with me, then?'

'John Perking came to see you on the morning of the day he killed his wife.'

'He did?' Dr Nayland evinced surprise. 'Well, you may be right. I've got a shocking memory for names.'

'For God's sake,' exploded Dover who wasn't finding the wooden bench the most comfortable seat in the world, 'you keep records, don't you?'

'Er – yes,' agreed Dr Nayland, looking round helplessly.

'Well, go and look at 'em!' Dover jerked his head at MacGregor who ushered Dr Nayland ahead of him, back into the surgery.

Dover closed his eyes and composed himself for forty winks. In a thoughtlessly short space of time MacGregor was back again.

'Three grubby cards in a shoe box!' he announced contemptuously.

Dr Nayland had trailed back behind him. 'Of course, mine is a private practice, you understand. I don't lumber myself up with all this National Health Service red tape.'

'We've managed to trace Perking, anyhow,' said MacGregor.

Dover grunted. 'Get on with it!'

'Come on, Nayland!' snapped MacGregor in his turn. 'Let's be hearing what this is all about.'

Dr Nayland tucked his cardboard box under one arm and sorted unhappily through a sheaf of letters which he had also brought with him. 'I don't know', he murmured, 'that this is quite ethical. Doctor-patient relationship, you know. Secrets of the confessional, and all that.'

Dover snorted.

Dr Nayland was offended. 'One still has one's principles, you know. One's Hippocratic oath, for instance.'

Dover's patience, unlike the widow's cruse, habitually ran out at an alarming speed. The seedy Dr Nayland had ceased to amuse him. In order that Dr Nayland himself should have cognizance of the situation Dover rose majestically to his feet and thrust his face close to that of the unfortunate medical practitioner. Dr Nayland recoiled.

'Listen, doc,' rasped Dover, 'don't try getting clever with me or I'll lean on you so hard you won't know what's hit you! When I ask you for information, spit it out quick, see? Otherwise I'll drag it out of you – teeth and all!'

Dr Nayland cringed.

'And don't give me any of that crap about your Hippocratic oath, either,' Dover continued heavily. 'If I'm any judge of character you kept your fingers crossed when you took it all right. This is a murder case and I'm in a hurry. Talk!'

'But, suppose this Perking man sues me?' whimpered Dr Nayland. 'Suppose the B.M.A. finds out? They'll chuck me out again and then what'll I do?'

'My heart's bleeding,' scoffed Dover, 'and your nose will be if you don't get a move-on.'

Dr Nayland shrugged his shoulders. 'What is it you want to know?'

Once Dover had achieved his capitulation he lost interest. He raised his eyebrows at MacGregor and slumped back on to his bench again. MacGregor, notebook and pencil at the ready, moved smartly forward. Like his master he had realized that

Dr Nayland was unlikely to stand up for his rights under common law or anything else.

'Is John Perking a regular patient of yours?' he demanded.

Dr Nayland sat down gingerly on another bench. 'No, not what you'd call regular. He rang me up—oh—about three weeks or so ago and asked me for an appointment. I—er—managed to squeeze him in that very lunch hour as a matter of fact. Sudden cancellation, you understand. Well, he duly arrived. I must admit I was a bit disappointed when I actually saw him. A rather common-looking young man. Not what you'd call officer material, don't you know. I made a point of mentioning my charge for a consultation right away. He seemed a little surprised at the amount but he didn't kick up any fuss about it. Which is more than you can say about some of them,' he added resentfully. 'I'd like to insist on payment in advance but it hardly seems ethical.'

MacGregor ignored the financial difficulties of the medical profession and returned to the point. 'This was Perking's first visit to you, was it?'

'Yes.'

'And what did he want to consult you about?'

Dr Nayland wriggled half-heartedly. 'This goes very much against the grain, I must say. I want it put on record that I'm only doing this under extreme pressure. Mr Perking consulted me about a very delicate and intimate matter.'

'Which was?'

'Well, he wanted to know if he was capable of fathering children.'

Dover and MacGregor exchanged glances. 'Sounds reasonable,' said Dover condescendingly.

Dr Nayland was furious. 'I don't know what that remark is supposed to mean but if it's an insinuation that I am expected to be lying I want it put on record that I entirely refute the implication.'

'I don't quite understand', said MacGregor, 'why Perking should consult you. Why didn't he go to his own doctor?'

Dr Nayland flung up his hands in despair. 'Because he

wanted his consultation on the quiet, that's why. It's understandable, isn't it? It's not the sort of thing any chap wants bandied around the town. In the normal course I should have sent him to the hospital for the tests but, in view of the circumstances, I did the preliminaries myself here.'

MacGregor stared at his notebook. 'And all this happened on his first visit? Three weeks ago?'

'That's right. Naturally I don't have the facilities for doing all the lab work here so I had to send the specimens to the hospital. I told him he'd have to wait a week or so but that I'd give him a ring when the results came through. Well, the other day I got the results from the hospital laboratory and I rang him up right away and suggested he should pop in and see me. He came round within – oh, a couple of hours or so.'

MacGregor had his mouth open to ask the next question but Dover got his in first. 'He gave you the name of John Perking, did he?'

'Yes, I've even got it written down here.' Dr Nayland fumbled in his shoe box. 'And he gave his address care of the Safari-Agogo Travel Agency and their phone number.'

'Funny,' said Dover, looking crossly at the doctor. 'You'd have thought he'd have given a false name, wouldn't you? I mean, since he'd gone to all this trouble to consult a strange doctor and everything.'

Dr Nayland understood the point very well. 'Mind you, I had to get in touch with him when the lab results came through. You never know how long these things are going to take. It might be a week or it might be six. It wouldn't be on, would it? – me ringing up this travel agency and asking for Mr Smith.'

'No,' agreed Dover glumly. 'Perhaps you've got something there.'

'Besides,' added Dr Nayland, 'I didn't know him from Adam anyhow.'

'You must be about the only person in Pott Winckle who doesn't,' groused Dover and switched himself off again.

MacGregor looked at the Chief Inspector and, on the evidence of the closed eyes, the sagging jowl and the heavy breathing, concluded that he could resume the questioning.

'The second time Perking came to see you, what was his manner like?'

'Well,' said Dr Nayland, wrinkling his brow in thought, 'I seem to remember he was pretty much on edge when he came in. Apprehensive. You can hardly blame him, can you? Rotten thing for a chap to have hanging over him. He took it very badly when I told him. Seemed to think it was my fault. He got quite nasty about it. Just for a minute I thought he was going to belt me one. In the end I had to let him read the lab report before he'd calm down. He didn't understand it, of course. They never do, but, if a bit of medical jargon gives 'em any comfort, let 'em have it – that's what I think.'

MacGregor's pencil hovered in mid-air. 'But, what was the lab report?'

Dr Nayland sighed and with a gesture of exasperation snatched up one of the letters from the pile he was still clutching. He rattled off a selection of its contents. 'There! And now, are you any the wiser?'

MacGregor shook his head.

'Well, if you want the answer in words of one syllable – negative.'

'Negative?'

'That's right. Nobody would ever call him Daddy.'

'But … ' MacGregor's mouth dropped in astonishment. 'There must be some mistake.'

Dr Nayland smiled gently. 'That's what he kept saying. No, no mistake. Mind you, there's a faint chance that with treatment … But, frankly, I wouldn't be too optimistic. I didn't tell him that, though. We medicos try to paint as cheerful a picture as we can. Even', he added sardonically, 'when the poor mutts are evidently in extremis.'

'Never mind about that for the moment,' said MacGregor hurriedly. 'Let's get this quite clear. As of this moment Perking is incapable of fathering a child?'

'That is correct.'

'But, how long has he been like this?'

'Oh, all his life. Or at least since puberty, that is.'

'You mean he never, at any time, could get a woman pregnant?'

'He is totally incapable of it and always has been. That clear enough for you?'

In his bewilderment MacGregor turned to Dover for support and guidance. He should have known better. The Chief Inspector's unlovely head was sunk low on his chest, his arms were loosely folded over his softly rising and falling stomach. From his lips a faint bubbling sound emerged.

MacGregor glowered at him. Really, this was too much! He stiffened the forefinger of his right hand and mercilessly jabbed it into the fatty layer which covered Dover's ribs. Dover, the target area being protected by an overcoat which would probably have stopped a bullet, grunted and twitched his moustache. MacGregor, his impatience making him brutal, struck again.

'Ughoogaahumph!' slobbered Dover. His huge frame wobbled but did not wake.

MacGregor, now almost beside himself, bellowed down Dover's ear. 'Sir!'

Dover opened one eye cautiously. 'Uh?'

'Did you hear what Dr Nayland said, sir?' demanded MacGregor, jaws clenched.

'Eh?' Dover blinked, stared round him in a bemused manner and stretched himself stiffly. 'These benches aren't half hard!' He glared belligerently at his sergeant. 'Course I heard what he said. Why the blazes shouldn't I?'

'Well, what do you think about it, sir?' asked MacGregor maliciously.

Dover scowled. He'd pay the young so-and-so out for this, by God he would! Cheeky devil! Since he could not, for the moment, vent his wrath on MacGregor, Dover turned with unerring instinct to vent it on Dr Nayland. 'Now, look here, What's-your-name,' he growled, 'just watch what you're saying! I've had people trying to box clever with me before and they've lived to regret it. Now, I'm going to give you a second chance. I'm going to forget all you said before so you can start with a clean slate. If you want to add or retract anything, now's the time to do it.'

Dr Nayland looked at Dover. Then, getting no help from a close scrutiny of that flabby countenance, he looked at Mac-Gregor. 'What the hell does he want me to say?' he asked in a despairing whisper.

'Tell him what you told me about Perking,' hissed Mac-Gregor, realizing that he'd been outplayed.

'Perking was sterile,' Dr Nayland obliged. 'Can't father kids. Not', he bethought himself cheerfully, 'that that's going to bother him much if he's going down for a twenty-year stretch'.

Dover digested the information and then pronounced his considered judgment. 'Poppycock!'

Dr Nayland bridled. 'It isn't!'

'Must be,' said Dover flatly.

'But, dammit, it's all down here in black and white.'

Dover flapped the lab report away. 'They must have made a mistake.'

'Of course they haven't made a mistake! They don't make mistakes like that.'

'I don't suppose it'd be the first time,' Dover observed darkly.

'Oh, look here,' – Dr Nayland sat down on the bench next to Dover – 'you've really got to be sensible about this. The lab report is correct. It must be. Besides, look at Perking's history. He's been married nearly three years and nothing's happened. That shows you there was something wrong, doesn't it?'

'Look, doc,' said Dover, happy to be able to put Dr Nayland and the entire medical profession if needs be in their place, 'Perking's wife was two months pregnant when she was killed. She'd been told that definitely by her own doctor that very morning.'

Dr Nayland looked annoyed. 'Maybe *her* lab tests were wrong,' he suggested nastily.

'The pregnancy was confirmed at the post mortem. See?' Dover crowed in cheap triumph.

Dr Nayland responded with a knowing laugh. 'All right, the wife may have been pregnant but that doesn't mean that the husband's responsible, does it? You must have led a very sheltered life, Chief Inspector. I didn't know you bogies were so pure-minded.'

A dark red flush of fury diffused Dover's face. A reflection on the honour of Cynthia Perking was a reflection on the honour of Daniel Wibbley. And a reflection on the honour of Daniel Wibbley was a reflection on the honour of Dover's prospective employer. Dover suddenly felt very indignant and very loyal. He swung round to Dr Nayland, clamped two beefy hands on the lapels of his white coat and drew him menacingly close.

'Take my advice, Nayland, and keep that lip of yours buttoned up! You can get into serious trouble going round slandering people, and trouble, laddie,' – Dover dragged Dr Nayland a couple of inches nearer – 'is that you would do well to avoid. One more scurrilous crack out of you about a poor girl who's dead and can't defend herself and I'll bust this little racket of yours here wide open! Get it? A few judicious inquiries round this part of the world and you'd find yourself up the creek without a paddle, wouldn't you, mate? However,' – Dover gave his victim a minatory shake – 'if you're a sensible fellow we might consider closing an official eye here and there. Understand? You scratch my back, laddie, and I might – I only say might, mind – I might just risk soiling my hands by scratching yours. Got it?'

Dr Nayland, released abruptly and sliding as fast as he could to the far end of the bench, gulped and nodded.

'Right,' said Dover approvingly, 'not another word about Cynthia Perking, eh? In fact, not a word about anything at all. That'll be safest. MacGregor, collect those cards and letters and things and let's get out of this dump.'

Chapter Thirteen

'But we can't just close our eyes and bury our heads in the sand, can we, sir?'

Dover placed two hands tenderly on the vast expanse of his stomach. 'Do you know, I think that fish was off. I've got a sort of shooting, searing pain right across here. Of course,' – he assumed his martyred air – 'God knows, fish doesn't have to be off to upset *me*.'

'We know Cynthia Perking was pregnant, sir, and we know her husband couldn't be the father.' MacGregor gallantly continued flogging a dead horse that was already eyeing its bed with interest.

Dover removed his jacket with a wince. 'My shoulder's still not right, you know. I reckon that little brute, Perking, broke something. A fractured collar bone, maybe?' He sat on the edge of his bed and began pushing his right boot off with his left foot.

'There's really only one explanation, sir, isn't there? Some other man must be the father.'

'My head feels rotten, too,' Dover observed to the room at large. 'I reckon he damaged my sight. I keep sort of getting black things floating in front of my eyes.'

'Even if Perking's lab report was wrong, sir,' sighed Mac-Gregor, prepared to concede a minor point, 'it doesn't make any difference, does it? If Perking only *thought* she had been unfaithful to him, that would give him motive enough, wouldn't it, sir? You've got to look at the timing, sir. Dr Nayland tells Perking he's sterile or whatever it is. Perking, absolutely shattered at the news, returns to his office. Almost immediately Mrs Perking rings him up and tells him she's expecting a baby. He broods over it all afternoon, decides he's going to kill her and tries to work out some sort of an alibi for himself. Then, when the travel agency closes, he cycles off home same as usual, and kills her.'

'I think I'll take my teeth out,' mused Dover. 'I've got a very funny sort of taste in my mouth.' He got up and padded over to the washbasin. While he filled a glass with water he examined his tongue despondently in the mirror.

MacGregor gave it up. It was like trying to reason with a bolster overstuffed with goose feathers. 'By the sound of it, sir,' he commented with an irony that was completely wasted, 'you'd be better off in bed.'

'Do you think so?' Dover gazed at MacGregor with a grateful eye. 'I never know when I've done enough, that's my trouble. They're always telling me I drive myself too hard.'

Further reassurance and encouragement stuck in MacGregor's throat but Dover had already allowed himself to be convinced.

'Well, just this once,' he said coyly. 'A couple of hours with my head down'll probably do me a world of good.'

'Yes, sir,' MacGregor agreed grimly. 'Well, I'll leave you to get your nap, sir.'

Dover's beady little black eyes snapped with suspicion. 'What are you going to do?'

MacGregor frowned. He'd hoped to get away without any questions. 'I did think I'd just pop in and see Cynthia Perking's doctor, sir?'

'Waffor?'

MacGregor shrugged his shoulders. 'Well, sir, something's gone wrong somewhere, hasn't it? Cynthia Perking's doctor might be able to throw some light, mightn't he? Lots of people treat their doctors as sort of father confessors. Suppose Mrs Perking was so set on having a baby that she – well – resorted to artificial insemination or something.'

Dover, snuggled down and getting nicely warm and cosy, contented himself with one brief four-letter word.

'Well, we've still got the contradiction, haven't we, sir? We've got a husband who's sterile and a wife who's pregnant.

There must be some explanation and, in my opinion, we could do with some more medical guidance.'

'Tell you what,' mumbled Dover sleepily, 'you go back and chat with the neighbours again.'

'Oh, sir!'

'It's got to be done, laddie. No use whining about it. Ask around. Maybe Cynthia Perking did have a gentleman friend after all.'

'But, sir, I've already done that twice and there's not a breath of scandal about her anywhere.'

'Don't let's spoil the ship for a ha'porth of your valuable time, laddie.' Dover yawned. 'You could make a few more inquiries about that dark-green car, too, while you're at it.'

MacGregor made a stand. 'Really, sir, I must protest! I just don't see the point of going over and over ground we've already covered. I do think that we ought to go and see Cynthia Perking's doctor. At least he might be able to tell us something new.' There was a muffled grunt from the pile of bedclothes. 'Sir?'

The pile of bedclothes heaved irritably. 'Are you still here?' came Dover's voice. 'Push off and let me get some rest!'

'But, Cynthia Perking's doctor, sir? I do think he ought to be interviewed, I really do.'

'So do I,' agreed Dover unexpectedly. 'In fact, I reckon I'll go and see him myself. In the morning.'

Many of Dover's overnight declarations did not survive the harsh light of the following morning, but this one was an exception. The Rolls came round, the two detectives stepped into it and MacGregor gave the chauffeur the address of Cynthia Perking's doctor.

MacGregor's expedition the previous afternoon back into the jungle of Birdsfoot-Trefoil Close had once again drawn a complete blank, as both Dover and MacGregor had known it would. Their reactions to the failure were, however, quite different. Dover was exuberant that he had pulled another fast one on his snooty young sergeant and MacGregor, his misbegotten afternoon still rankling, was sulking. Several of the ladies had completely misinterpreted the purpose of his repeated visits and at times it had been extremely embarrassing. Both Dover and MacGregor, however, were so occupied with their own thoughts that neither of them had bothered about phoning up their next interviewee to see if the time of their visit was convenient.

They arrived in the middle of morning surgery.

'Dr M'Gillooly certainly can't see you now.' The harassed-looking woman entrenched in a glorified cubby hole in the hallway shook her head. Her starched white overall crackled. 'I'm afraid I don't care who you are or where you've come from. You'll just have to wait your turn.'

MacGregor, in charge as usual of these mundane negotiations, found himself caught between Scylla and Charybdis.

Scylla administered an impatient and rather painful thump in the small of his underling's back. 'Get on with it, laddie! Tell the old cow we're going to see the doctor and if she doesn't like it she can lump it!' He didn't bother to lower his voice.

Charybdis drew herself up in a cold fury. 'Over my dead body!' she enunciated slowly.

'Suits me!' rumbled Scylla, trying to propel MacGregor forward by brute force.

MacGregor gazed appealingly at Charybdis.

Charybdis was unmoved. 'No,' she repeated, her prim Edinburgh accent getting full value out of the word. 'I absolutely forbid it.'

As he himself was wont to claim, Dover was a man of deeds not words. Faced with an immovable object he rather fancied himself as an irresistible force. War-war was often better than jaw-jaw. He'd tried being reasonable and courteous and where had it got him? Now it was time to act. With his feet. He walked forward.

MacGregor, a comparative lightweight, was swept aside. Charybdis made as if to leap across her counter and out of the cubby hole, a selfless victim to the Juggernaut. Then she had second thoughts and contented herself by saying, 'Well, really!' in a very disgusted voice.

'Which way?' demanded Dover as he passed.

Charybdis clamped her lips. Then she smiled in disagreeable anticipation. 'Through the waiting room. You'll see the notice on the door.'

'Ta,' said Dover sarcastically and flung open the door of the waiting room.

He was greeted by an expectant and inquisitive hush accompanied by a pungent whiff of eucalyptus. No less than forty pairs of eyes examined him, summed him up and, for the most part, dismissed him.

One or two judicious comments were however passed before the speakers reverted to the more interesting subject of their own and other people's ailments. 'Drunken brawl,' opined one uncharitable housewife to her neighbour. 'I think it's disgusting, letting the likes of them get treatment on the National Health.' An elderly man wheezed an alternative verdict. 'He'll not make old bones,' he chuckled. 'Fat as a pig. He wants to get some of that belly off him. If he don't' – he wheezed and chuckled at the same time – 'they'll be needing a double-decker box for him when his time comes.'

Luckily Dover was above such things. In any case his hearing wasn't as good as it might have been. He spotted the surgery door at the far end of the room and rolled purposefully towards it, towing MacGregor like a dinghy in his wake.

The atmosphere in the waiting room underwent a rapid change.

'In the queue, mate!' ordered a burly workman who wanted a few days' sick while he decorated the kitchen. He jerked his thumb eloquently at a couple of vacant chairs.

Dover haughtily ignored the proffered suggestion. He was nearly halfway towards his goal now. The waiting patients switched to more militant action. A wizened old lady gallantly thrust her walking stick out in an attempt to trip up the intruder. She was a fraction too late. A well-muscled young woman, temporarily abandoning her brood of six adenoidal

163

kids, rose from her seat by the surgery door. Arms akimbo, she barred Dover's way.

'Hey, cheeky! Where d'you think you're going?'

Dover hesitated. This was no nine-stone weakling. 'I want to see the doctor.'

'Watcher think we're doing then, eh? Waiting for a tram?'

'I happen to be on important official business, madam.' Dover managed a patronizing smile.

A rather surprising suggestion as to what he should do with his official business came from a neatly dressed female with a bad case of varicose veins and a nasty cold. Dover, mouth sagging in astonishment, made the tactical error of turning to look at her. When he turned back again he found that the living barrier had been reinforced. No less than six stalwart patients now stood resolute between him and the surgery door.

'There's the end of the queue,' said the Amazon, complacently watching her youngest brat slobber over Dover's left boot. 'We don't have no favouritism here.' The waiting room nodded its collective head in solemn agreement. 'First come first served and last come last served. I haven't been sitting here two solid hours to stand by like a muggins while somebody like you pushes in before me.'

'That's right!' A rheumy-eyed old fellow poked irritably at Dover with one of his two walking sticks. 'Back in line, sonnie!'

Dover took a step forward. The barrier stiffened and closed its ranks. The old man raised one stick defensively. Dover saw the chance of a cheap revenge and, to MacGregor's eternal shame, took it. His foot shot out and neatly kicked the old man's other stick away. The old man crashed to the floor with a howl of despair and all hell broke loose. Hitherto passive onlookers seized magazines from the waiting-room table, rolled them up and used them to belabour round the ears those who had dared to flout the most sacred of British traditions. In no time at all Dover was bitten, thumped, pushed and generally abused. MacGregor, only too eager to leave his master to the fate he had so richly asked for, found his own retreat cut off and tried vainly to protect his head and face with his arms.

The receptionist rushed in from the hall. Dr M'Gillooly and a stark-naked patient rushed in from the surgery. Gradually order and decorum were restored. Dover and MacGregor found themselves, resentful but chastened, sitting side by side on two chairs at the end of the queue. The other patients, breathless but triumphant, were eventually prevailed upon to resume their rightful places and interrupted conversations.

Dover and MacGregor didn't have more than an hour and a half to wait before they got Dr M'Gillooly all to themselves.

'I can't imagine', said Dr M'Gillooly tartly, 'why you had to come during surgery. You might have known I wouldn't have time to see you.'

'On murder inquiries', Dover told him with equal tartness, 'every second counts.'

'But I thought you'd already arrested your man? Don't tell me that, once again, the police have blundered. Both Mr Perking and his wife were patients of mine and I must say I find the idea that he murdered her in such a brutal manner quite ludicrous. They were a most affectionate couple and he always struck me as being a very decent fellow.'

'He struck me as being a thug and a sadist,' snarled Dover. He indicated the remains of his black eyes. 'Look what he did to me in an entirely uncalled-for and unprovoked attack. If I hadn't been pretty capable of looking after myself in a punch-up he might have killed me. An absolutely ungoverned temper, that's what Perking has.'

Dr M'Gillooly looked at the door leading to the waiting room and offered no comment. 'What was it you wanted to see me about?'

'Cynthia Perking's pregnancy,' said Dover. 'We're a bit puzzled about it.'

'I can't see why. It was all quite normal. Conception had been rather a long time coming but it had happened in the end. When she first came to see me I was pretty certain that she was pregnant, but at such an early stage one can't always be sure. However, one can carry out a perfectly simple test and this is, in fact, precisely what I did. When the results came back they proved that Mrs Perking was pregnant and when she came to see me on the morning of the day she was killed, I told her so. Poor girl, she was so thrilled.'

'I believe', said MacGregor, 'that she had consulted you earlier about her inability to conceive.'

'That is correct. I arranged a full examination. There was absolutely nothing wrong with her and I told her so.'

'And her husband?'

Dr M'Gillooly sighed. 'Well, obviously, one would have liked to examine him as well. It was the only logical thing to do. However, without his consent and co-operation, my hands were tied. Mrs Perking told me that he absolutely refused to come in for an examination and, indeed, that he was so touchy about the whole subject that he wouldn't even come in and have a chat with me. Some men are like that, you know. It was a pity but one could understand his attitude in a way. A man does have his pride.'

'Would you', asked MacGregor, venturing to continue the questioning as Dover seemed to have lost interest, 'be surprised to hear that John Perking did in fact consult another doctor on the question of his sterility?'

Dr M'Gillooly pursed his lips. 'No, not really. These things are often easier to discuss with a stranger. A strange doctor? No, that does not surprise me. Which doctor was it, by the way?'

'Dr Nayland.'

'Oh.' Dr M'Gillooly raised his eyebrows.

'You know him?'

'Only by reputation,' admitted Dr M'Gillooly cautiously.

'A right shifty little burk,' Dover commented sourly. 'He's up to no good, if you ask me.'

'I'm afraid I can't pass any opinion on that judgment, Mr Dover.' Dr M'Gillooly smiled in embarrassment. 'A fellow practitioner, you understand.'

'Load of old cod's wallop, that,' said Dover. 'Downright

dishonest, if you ask me—covering up for a scoundrel just because he's a colleague. Catch me turning a blind eye where a crooked copper's concerned! I'd jump on him soon as look at him, I would.' Dover smiled grimly at the prospect. 'It'd be my duty, see?'

'Er—quite,' said Dr M'Gillooly. He turned back to Mac-Gregor. 'Is there anything else? I have rather a large visiting list to get through this afternoon.'

'Is Dr Nayland a competent man, do you think, sir?'

Dr M'Gillooly frowned. There were some subjects one preferred not to keep harping on. 'I have no reason to think that he is not.'

'He told John Perking—and us, too, if it comes to that—that Perking was sterile.'

'Oh,' said Dr M'Gillooly, and thought about it.

'Does that surprise you, sir?'

'Well, yes, I suppose it does, really.' His frown deepened. 'Mrs Perking, I do assure you, was pregnant. Of course, there could have been another man, I suppose.'

'Did she give you any hint that that might be the situation?'

'No, rather the reverse. As I told you, she was wildly delighted when I told her that she was pregnant. She was laughing and said she hoped it was a boy and she'd insist on it being called John after her husband—the sort of things any excited young wife would say in similar circumstances. I must confess I find it hard to believe that she was pregnant by another man.'

'How about artificial insemination?'

Dr M'Gillooly sighed. These television programmes had a lot to answer for. 'Quite out of the question.' He looked at his watch. 'I'm afraid you will just have to accept my assurance on that point. I haven't time to explain but the legal, moral and medical aspects are extremely complicated and I am absolutely certain that no arrangements of that kind could possibly have been made without my knowledge—to say nothing of the fact that the husband's prior cognizance and consent is a sine qua non.'

MacGregor was beginning to acquire a haunted look. 'Well, how do you explain it, doctor?'

'Luckily I don't have to. It could, I suppose, have been some chance, fleeting encounter with a perfect stranger. One has heard of childless wives resorting in desperation to that sort of thing. She may even have convinced herself that such an encounter never took place and that the child was, in fact, her husband's. One has known stranger cases of self-deception.'

'Could Dr Nayland have mistaken Perking's condition?'

'I should have hardly thought so. Besides, the diagnosis would be based on tests made at a laboratory. Apart from actually telling the patient I shouldn't have thought Dr Nayland himself would have had much say in the matter.'

MacGregor handed over the letter which he had taken from Dr Nayland. Dr M'Gillooly read it.

'Well, that's that, isn't it?' He handed the letter back. 'And now I must really ask you to excuse me.'

'Just a minute!' Dover scratched his head and the dandruff fell in its habitual shower on the shoulders of his overcoat. 'This laboratory everybody keeps talking about – where is it?'

'It's attached to our general hospital, here in Pott Winckle. But a mistake on the lab's part is quite out of the question. Everything they do is checked and double-checked. I have used them for many, many years and I have always found them absolutely reliable.'

Dover chewed his lip and then screwed his little finger deep in his left ear. Dr M'Gillooly watched him with some distaste.

'Wax,' explained Dover, holding out his finger in proof.

'Indeed?' said Dr M'Gillooly coldly.

'I reckon I need 'em syringing out.' Dover smiled hopefully.

Dr M'Gillooly smiled politely back. 'You should consult your own doctor.' He consulted his watch yet again. 'Now, I really must … '

'When you examined Mrs Perking for pregnancy, what did you do exactly?'

'Oh, really!' Dr M'Gillooly seethed with impatience.

'You needn't go through the whole rigmarole,' said Dover

obligingly—he was not unaware that lunch-time was drawing near, 'but I thought you or somebody said something about making some tests.'

'That is correct. One takes a sample of blood which is then injected into a rabbit and ... '

'Do you do all that?'

'Of course not. I send the blood samples to the laboratory.'

'The same laboratory?'

Dr M'Gillooly's forehead creased in another frown. 'Well, yes, the same laboratory.'

Chapter Fourteen

DOVER didn't make the same mistake twice. At least, not on this occasion. Immediately after lunch MacGregor was dispatched to phone up the local hospital and make an appointment with the director of the laboratory while Dover, top trouser-button undone, concentrated on his digestive processes.

MacGregor walked slowly back across the hotel lounge. He was not feeling particularly happy. What was there about Pott Winckle that made the Chief Inspector so reluctant to leave? MacGregor couldn't for the life of him imagine. Maybe Mrs Dover was making life uncomfortable for her spouse in Acacia Avenue? Maybe Dover's sister-in-law had come to stay again? Or, perhaps, was it Scotland Yard itself that Dover was giving a wide berth to? The Assistant Commissioner (Crime) was inclined to go into apoplexy at the mere sight of the Metropolitan Police's most unwanted man. Maybe he had issued an ultimatum: get out and stay out? It wouldn't, MacGregor reflected glumly, be the first time.

Well, thought MacGregor – his heart sinking as he caught sight of the semi-recumbent source of all his trouble – nobody but a fool would accept Dover's own justification for this shameless waste of public time and money. It might be true that Dover rejoiced to see the guilty get more than they deserved but that didn't mean he was going to exert himself to see that they did. He'd talk until the cows came home about bringing back the thumbscrew and the rack, but that's as far as it went. All this guff about insuring that there would be no sloppy sympathy for Perking either at his trial or later cut no ice with MacGregor. A fat lot Dover really cared! Anybody who thought of Dover in the role of a crusader for justice wanted his head examining. MacGregor grinned at the mental picture this idea evoked. Dover, rolling along in full armour and in one of those little nightshirt things, waving a ...

'What the blazes are you sniggering about?'

MacGregor came to with a start. 'Oh, nothing, sir. I was just thinking.'

Dover rolled his eyes towards the ceiling of the hotel lounge. 'I've been lumbered with some stupid ginks of sergeants in my time but you take the flaming biscuit! You'll be talking to yourself before long and you know what that means, don't you? They'll be coming for you in a plain van, laddie.'

'I shouldn't be surprised, sir,' said MacGregor.

Dover grunted. He had a sneaking suspicion that his sergeant was being cheeky but post-prandial somnolence was rapidly setting in. Dover yawned. 'Well?'

'Well what, sir?'

'Did you get through to this laboratory place, you damned fool? That's what you went for, isn't it?'

'Yes, sir. The director will be free to see us any time this afternoon. I said we'd probably be around in about ten minutes.'

'We're not in that much of a hurry,' grumbled Dover.

'I'm sorry, sir. I thought you said you didn't want to give them time to cook the books. I must have misunderstood you.'

Dover eyed MacGregor suspiciously. Was that another crack? That was the trouble with these blooming lah-di-dah types. You never knew if they were trying to get a rise out of you or whether it was just the way they spoke. 'Well', said Dover, a bit defensively, 'it stands to reason, doesn't it? The lab must have made a mistake about Perking.'

MacGregor sighed. 'Probably, sir.'

'I don't trust the medical profession,' Dover continued moodily. 'If they didn't all hang together, there'd be a good few of 'em hanging separately, believe me! And if they're prepared to cover up criminals amongst their ranks, they're not going to jib at white-washing a bit of the old incompetence, are they? Oh, I could tell you a few things about doctors and suchlike that'd make your hair stand on end. The things I've suffered at their hands with my stomach – I could write a book about it.'

MacGregor was spared further painful revelations by the timely arrival of their chauffeur. He marched through the swing doors of the hotel and stood, waiting respectfully, with his cap under his arm.

Dover wrinkled his nose. Back to the old grindstone! 'Tell that lackey to hang on a minute,' he instructed MacGregor. 'Before we go, you nip off to the phone again and find out what time the trains are back to London. I shouldn't think we'll be messing about long at this laboratory place.'

'You mean – go back to London this afternoon, sir?'

'Why not? We're finished here, aren't we? We've solved their blooming case for them, haven't we? What more do you want, for God's sake? I'm only going to this lab just to settle the odd point for my own satisfaction. We might have a bit of fun with 'em, too,' he added with a spiteful grin, 'if there has been a slip-up. I'll put the fear of God into 'em, you see if I don't. Well, come on, laddie! Don't stand there like a stuffed lemon with duck's disease!'

'Are you going to see Mr Wibbley again before we leave, sir?'

'I should co-co!' sneered Dover. 'Who does Mr Wibbley think he is when he's at home, anyhow? He's just a big fish in a little pond, that's all he is. And don't say anything to that chauffeur fellow. We'll come back here and pack and get a taxi to the station.'

'The Chief Constable, sir?' asked MacGregor, not unused to these ignominious and furtive retreats from the scenes of crimes they had been sent to solve.

'Stuff him!'

The Rolls-Royce set them down outside the main entrance to the hospital. Dover boggled at the enormous flight of granite steps which rose steeply before them. 'What happens if you've broken your bloody leg?' he demanded.

'Oh, I expect they'd carry you up on a stretcher, sir.'

Dover snorted and laboriously began his climb.

'Oh, look, sir!'

Sullenly Dover followed the line of MacGregor's pointing finger. A big black cat was leisurely making its way from one side of the steps to the other. As Dover glowered at it it sat down and raised one fat front paw to its mouth.

' 'Strewth!' said Dover.

'No, hang on a minute, sir! If we give it a chance it might walk right across in front of us.'

Dover, not unwilling to rest his aching feet and straining lungs, could not however repress his innermost thoughts. 'Have you gone completely off your rocker?'

'It's a black cat, sir, and we could do with a bit of luck, couldn't we? Look, sir, it's getting up now. Come on, pussikins, there's a good little pussy-wussy! I think it's going to walk across, sir. Yes, there it goes! That's a good old pussy!'

'Well, swelp me!' said Dover.

'Oh, you'll see, sir,' — MacGregor smiled fatuously at the cat — 'that'll bring us good luck, that will. He walked right across in front of us. Do you know, sir,' — MacGregor, taking the steps two at a time, had somewhat outstripped his Chief Inspector — 'I wouldn't be surprised if we don't crack this case wide open.'

'It's cracked wide open now, you damned fool!' panted Dover. 'And after that little exhibition of yours, nothing would surprise me!'

The entrance hall was vast, echoing and empty, except for a distraught-looking girl behind the reception desk. She was quite pretty so MacGregor turned on his most winsome smile. The girl gazed at him intently as he began to explain what he wanted. He'd hardly got more than a couple of words out before she was round from the back of her desk and clutching excitedly at his arm.

'Die Polizei? You are really the policemens? Gott sei dank! You are very quick. This way! This way!' She tightened her grip on MacGregor's arm and began dragging him across the entrance hall. 'We take the lift,' she explained breathlessly. 'Ach, gut! It now comes down.'

By the time the lift arrived Dover had also ambled across. 'What it is to have sex appeal!' he sneered.

MacGregor wasn't given time to work out some equally witty comeback. The lift came down and with a click the automatic doors slid back. There was one occupant inside. He was in a wheelchair and not very good at it. With both legs encased in huge plaster casts he edged awkwardly to and fro in an effort to get through doors which would have presented no obstacle to a Sherman tank, being wide enough for a stretcher or a coffin. MacGregor's girl friend exploded into a Teutonic fury at this display of ineptitude. She let fly a stream of hysterical curses at the thickly bandaged head of the man in the wheelchair.

The man in the wheelchair, not unnaturally, took exception. He stopped even trying to get out of the lift and with bandaged hands clamped firmly on the plaster-cast knees began to send back as good as he'd got.

With a banshee howl of rage MacGregor's girl friend shot into the lift, grabbed hold of the wheelchair, swung it round until it was pointing in the right direction, and pulled it towards her. 'Verdammte Kranke!' she screamed. And shoved.

Dover and MacGregor stepped neatly to one side as the wheelchair went by. They turned with interest to watch its headlong progress but long before it reached the distant wall they were unceremoniously hauled into the lift.

'You are together, yes?' The nurse-receptionist was already pressing the top button. 'I telephone them you are coming,' she added and leapt gracefully out through the closing doors.

For a moment Dover and MacGregor stood in silence as the lift moved slowly and carefully upwards.

'Just what', asked Dover with a mildness and reasonableness that boded ill for somebody, 'the purple blazes is going on here?'

'Well, I'm afraid I don't quite know, sir.' MacGregor watched the indicator light moving gradually from one number to the next. It was better than meeting Dover's blood-shot eye.

'You could have asked, couldn't you, you damned fool?'

'Well, she didn't really give me much chance, sir,' said MacGregor unhappily. 'I think she was some kind of foreigner.'

'I can see how you got in the detective branch!' muttered Dover.

The top floor came at last. The lift stopped and the doors opened.

'God help us,' groaned Dover, 'here's another one!'

Over the starched apron and under the starched cap two large eyes rolled ecstatically in a dusky face.

'You is da policeman?' White teeth flashed. 'Dis way, gennelmun! Follow me!'

'Look, just a minute,' began MacGregor but the nurse was halfway down the corridor and seemingly deaf to all entreaties. He turned helplessly to Dover.

'Oh, come on!' snarled Dover. 'We might as well follow her. If this is the National Health Service I'm going private next time. You and your bloody black cats!'

The coloured nurse was putting speed on. 'Hurry, man, hurry!' she shouted back at them and promptly disappeared through a door.

Dover and MacGregor, in Dover's own good time, eventually followed her. They found themselves in some sort of small storeroom in which all the space not occupied by neatly stacked bedpans and commodes was filled with a chattering excited mob of people. A man in a white overall fought his way through the crowd.

'Are you the police? Thank God for that!' With some difficulty he extricated one hand and mopped his brow. 'I thought you were never coming.'

Dover shoved MacGregor out of the way. The time for finesse and polite usage had long since gone. A fat sister screamed in anguish as MacGregor's foot crunched down on hers. Dover elbowed a Chinese probationer out of his way and seized the man in the white coat by the lapels. 'Are you in charge here?' he bellowed.

The man thought about it. 'Well, I suppose I'm the senior officer present but I can't possibly accept any responsibility.'

'Well, who the blazes are you?' screamed Dover, grabbing his bowler hat before it disappeared for ever in the throng.

'I'm the director of the laboratory,' explained the man in the white coat hoarsely. 'God, this is terrible! My name is Moreton. Dr Moreton.'

'Pleased to meet you, I'm sure,' snarled Dover, struggling to keep his feet as a surge, apparently starting over by the window, threatened to overwhelm him.

A wiry little Indian girl was fighting her way across the room. Dover grunted as somebody's elbow bored its way into his stomach. The Indian girl reached Dr Moreton, her cap askew and her apron torn.

'She is still there, sir,' she reported breathlessly and with unconcealed relish.

Dr Moreton didn't appear pleased with the news. 'God damn and rot the blasted woman!' he moaned. 'I've got a heavy work schedule planned for this afternoon, and then this has to go and happen. Some people have absolutely no consideration. Look here, constable,' – he turned with a shocking lack of tact to Dover – 'I think we'd better get out of here. You can't hear yourself think in this place. Like the tower of Babel! If you can shove your way through to the door, I'll follow you.'

Dover shoved. MacGregor shoved. Dr Moreton shoved. Several weaklings disappeared, presumably for ever, into the heaving mob. Outside the door they found another nascent herd assembling, all eager to join in the fun and all talking at the tops of their voices in unintelligible foreign languages.

Dr Moreton staggered down the corridor and propped himself up against the wall. 'I must be dreaming,' he said weakly. 'This is just a nightmare. I shall wake up soon.'

Dover brushed these rambling remarks aside. 'What's going on?' he demanded.

'You might well ask, constable, you might well ask!'

Dover was never one to get his priorities wrong. He grabbed Dr Moreton yet again by the lapels and shook him vigorously. 'If you call me constable again, laddie, I'll ram your teeth down your throat! I'm a bloody Detective Chief Inspector and if you know which side your bread's buttered on you'll remember it!' He released his hold on Dr Moreton's jacket in such a way that his head struck the wall with quite a loud thwack. Dr Moreton accepted the assault without protest. After what he'd gone through, who cared about the odd bump? 'Now,' thundered Dover, 'for the last time, what's going on in this mad house?'

'It's my fool of a secretary,' explained Dr Moreton, rubbing the back of his head. 'She was in the office just now—about half an hour ago—and she answered the telephone. As far as I was able to tell it was a perfectly ordinary sort of call— something about somebody wanting to come and see me. Anyhow, ordinary sort of call or not, as soon as she put the phone down she went berserk.' Dr Moreton pondered over his choice of words. 'Yes, I think that's an accurate description: she went berserk. My laboratory is in a sort of wooden hut thing out at the back of the hospital,' he went on. 'We've been promised new buildings—the working conditions are quite deplorable, you know—but I'll believe that when I see them. Well, she shot out of the laboratory building and raced across here to the main building. I saw her from the office window. No hat, no coat, nothing. It was tippling down, too, absolutely tippling. Well, I didn't know what to do. I suppose I should have run after her but ... ' He shrugged his shoulders. 'You never know what to do with women when they fly off the handle like that, do you? Well, I just stood there at the window for about five minutes or so, thinking she might just—well— sort of run back again and there'd be some perfectly reason- able explanation and that would be that. Then I saw the nurses starting to come across to the hospital from their quar- ters. They change shifts at half past two, you know. Well, I was still standing there watching them, you know how it is, when I saw one or two of them start looking up at the top floor of the hospital – where we are now, as a matter of fact. Then they started pointing and before you could say Florence Nightingale there was a whole crowd of them, squawking away like a farmyard full of hens. Oh, I knew then what it was – what it must be.' He chewed his thumbnail in anguish. 'I had a premonition, you see. Well, I left my office and went outside to see what all the fuss was about. Of course as soon as they saw me they all came twittering round like a flock of blooming sparrows and it was ages before I could get to the bottom of it. Then I found one young lady who could speak reasonable English – and that was a piece of luck – and I looked where she was pointing and, damn me, there she was!'

'There who was?' asked Dover.

'Mildred, my secretary. Who else? She'd climbed out on to the roof of the hospital, right up on top, you understand. Made my flesh creep just to see her. Well, the next thing we saw was a lot of heads poking out of the windows. It looked as though the entire staff of the hospital, to say nothing of the patients, had got wind of what had happened and … '

'Hang on a minute,' Dover interrupted him. 'Can't you cut it short a bit?' The Chief Inspector didn't go much on standing around in draughty corridors.

Dr Moreton looked annoyed. In certain medical circles he had quite a reputation as a raconteur. 'She's still out there,' he said, jerking his head sulkily, 'standing on a piece of decaying guttering, midway between two windows and out of reach of both of them. In answer to inquiries she says she is going to kill herself and she threatens that if anybody tries to get out on the roof with her she'll jump.'

Dover slumped against the wall and brooded over what he had been told. Down the corridor the comings and goings, the chirruping, the excited girlish giggles continued unabated. Who was looking after the patients, for God's sake? Suddenly his face brightened. That just showed you how run down he must be, didn't it? All this had damn-all to do with him! He was investigating a murder case.

'Well,' he observed cheerfully, 'it's all very interesting but it's not my affair, thank God! Now, do you think we could go back to your office because I've got a few questions to ask you and it's not very convenient here, is it?' He scowled at the pack of nurses. 'Too much blooming noise.'

Dr Moreton didn't understand. Dover, getting brusque, explained.

'But I can't just clear off and leave her out there on the roof!' protested Dr Moreton, showing considerable horror at the mere suggestion. 'She is my secretary, after all.'

'I don't give a hoot if she's your grandmother!' snapped Dover. 'If she wants to jump, let her! I haven't got time to waste hanging around while a nutcase like that makes her blooming mind up.'

'You don't mean that, I'm sure,' said Dr Moreton with a fatuous smile. 'I'm certain that if a kindly, fatherly sort of man like you were to have a few words with her she'd soon come back to her senses. I'll bet you've talked potential suicides round dozens of times in your career. It just needs somebody with the knack, that's all.'

'You', said Dover with unpardonable bluntness, 'must be as stupid as you look. I've got more important things to do than spend my time chatting up dizzy birds on roofs.' He chuckled. 'Hey, MacGregor, did you hear that? If you'd any sense you'd be making a note of some of these things I say. You'd make a fortune if you put 'em all together in a book.'

MacGregor had been listening to the conversation between Dover and Dr Moreton with growing embarrassment. He was accustomed to Dover's complete callousness but he knew it was liable to shock outsiders. He drew Dover to one side and made an appeal to his better nature.

'You know what the general public are like, sir,' he whispered. 'They like to look upon us policemen as their friends.'

'More fools them!' scoffed Dover.

'Suppose it gets in the newspapers, sir? And they say that you, a senior Scotland Yard detective, were on the spot and didn't do anything to help? The Commissioner would be livid, sir. You know how he feels about public relations.'

Dover scowled. 'If she's going to jump, she'll jump, won't she?' he grumbled. 'And if she isn't, she won't. There's nothing I can do about it.'

'You could *try*, sir.'

'And suppose I go and natter at her and off she pops, eh? They'll blame it all on me, won't they? That won't do our public image much bloody good, will it?'

'Well, will you let me have a shot at it, sir?'

Dover liked this idea even less. 'I'll give her five minutes', he announced generously, 'and that's all.' He glared at Dr Moreton. 'What's her blasted name?'

'Mildred,' obliged Dr Moreton quickly, 'Mildred Denny. She's a cousin of that girl who was murdered the other day. I don't know if that's what's upset her.'

Chapter Fifteen

To THOSE who only know Chief Inspector Dover in his lethargic, permanently-hibernating-dormouse mood, his reaction to Dr Moreton's casual remark would come as a revelation. Bouncing with fury he bawled orders in all directions – orders which when they weren't unintelligible were contradictory. MacGregor and Dr Moreton scuttled hither and thither in panic-stricken attempts to round up the skittish nurses and clear them out of the storeroom. The nurses and the assorted medical auxiliaries who had manœuvred themselves into seats in the front row were loath to relinquish them and a couple of hospital porters actually squared up to MacGregor and asked him how he'd like a punch up the nose.

'Why wasn't I told?' screamed Dover, getting very red and very hoarse. 'Why wasn't I told? I'm surrounded by certifiable cretins, that's what it is!' He seized his bowler hat and in an excess of emotion rammed it even further down on his head.

MacGregor, looking shop-worn, panted up to report. 'We've got the room cleared, sir, but it'd take a company of guardsmen with fixed bayonets to shift 'em off the top floor. They're all leaning out of the other storeroom windows and as soon as we move them out of one room they pick another lock and fill up another.'

'Moron!' snarled Dover. 'Call yourself a copper? I've seen better policemen than you in mouldy cheese.'

'If you'd like to come this way, sir,' said MacGregor, nobly turning the other cheek, 'I think we can get you through. If you'd just stick close behind me, sir.'

They charged in tandem through the closely-packed ranks of interested spectators. In answer to MacGregor's warning yell Dr Moreton opened the storeroom door at exactly the right moment. As soon as the two policemen were safely inside the door was slammed to and a couple of large packing cases were dragged across to form a barricade.

Dover looked round for something to gripe about. He found it. 'Who's that?'

'This is Mr Whitbread, the hospital chaplain,' said Dr Moreton. 'We thought he might be able to help.'

'C. of E.,' said Mr Whitbread with a toothy smile. 'I'm quite prepared to go out there, you know. I haven't much of a head for heights and I may be the grandfather of our little party here, but I'm quite prepared to go out there.' He smoothed down his shock of snow-white hair.

Dover ignored him. 'Where is she, the bitch?'

'You'll have to lean right out of this window, sir,' Mac-Gregor explained, 'and sort of twist yourself round and upwards to your left. You'll see her standing on the roof six or seven feet above you.'

'I'll deal with you later,' Dover informed him as he pushed past and headed for the already open window. Carefully removing his bowler hat he stuck his head out and got a faceful of rain for his trouble. He looked down into the courtyard, which was a mistake because the hospital was a Victorian building of imposing height. Dover clung, limpet-like, to the window still.

'You'll have to lean further out than that, sir, or you won't be able to see her.'

Dover risked another inch and took a quick glance upwards. Thanks to the overhang of the roof he couldn't see anything. He pulled back into the room. 'I think she's jumped,' he said with ill-concealed relief. 'I can't see her.'

MacGregor had a look. 'No, sir, she's still there. You'll have to lean right out, sir. Perhaps if I held on to your legs … ?'

Mr Whitbread broke off his prayers. 'I'm quite prepared to have a go, you know. Quite prepared. My arthritis is hardly worrying me at all today, in spite of the inclement weather.'

Dover addressed MacGregor. 'You hold on to the tails of

my overcoat, and just see you hold on hard. If you let me slip ... ' He left the threat unfinished.

MacGregor gripped two handfuls of Dover's coat as the Chief Inspector poked his torso gingerly out of the window again. As he took the weight of Dover's seventeen and a quarter stone he was tempted. He would hardly have been human if he hadn't. However the presence of witnesses prevented the thought from fathering the deed.

Dover could now see a pair of rain-sodden shoes. That was good enough for him. He filled his lungs and let fly.

'Hey!'

The rain-sodden shoes leapt a good four inches into the air. There was a shriek of alarm. A couple of tiles hurtled down past Dover's window. The guttering sagged frighteningly as the rain-sodden shoes crashed back on to it.

'Her nerves must be in a shocking state,' muttered Dover. He addressed the shoes again. 'Are you all right up there, miss?'

Inside the room MacGregor shuddered fastidiously. The old fool had about as much delicacy and tact as a pregnant water-buffalo.

A mixture of a sniff and a sob came from the roof. 'I'm going to kill myself,' Mildred Denny called down. 'If anybody tries to come near me I shall jump at once.'

And the sooner the better, thought Dover crossly, but he made an effort and spoke in a voice which was meant to be kindly. 'Why don't you tell me all about it, eh?'

'Why should I?' retorted Mildred ungraciously.

'Well, I might be able to help you,' Dover replied, wheedling away like mad. 'I'm a very understanding chap.'

'You don't belong to the hospital, do you?' asked Mildred with marked suspicion.

'No, no!' Dover assumed an airy tone. 'I just – er – happened to be passing by and I thought I might be able to help.'

'You're a policeman,' said Mildred flatly.

Dover decided it was time to take a break and ducked back

inside the room. 'She's rumbled me,' he announced, mopping his dripping face. 'And, if you ask me, there'll soon be no need for her to jump through the pearly gates. If she stops out there much longer she'll be dead of pneumonia. It's raining cats and dogs.'

Mr Whitbread sidled forward, wringing his hands. 'Poor soul, poor soul!' he intoned. 'I do wish you'd let me climb there and bring her what consolations I can. Of course,' – he smiled his martyr's smile – 'you'll have to give me a leg up over the sill. My gammy knee, you know. Still got a bit of shrapnel in it from the North African desert.'

Dover, whose standards of personal hygiene were deplorable, sneezed loudly and all over Mr Whitbread. The cleric beat a hasty retreat to the back of the room and began praying vigorously in a less germ-laden atmosphere.

MacGregor pricked up his ears. 'I think she's calling, sir.'

Dover sighed and leaned out through the window again. 'Well?'

'You oughtn't to leave me alone,' said Mildred resentfully. 'I need help.'

'You need a damned good smack on the bottom,' Dover informed her, and meant it.

'What'll they do to me?' whined Mildred.

'I dunno,' said Dover. 'Who?'

'The police, of course. I'm a murderer, you know.'

'Oh, yes?' Dover had heard this sort of stuff a dozen times before and blandly discounted it.

'It was all my fault,' whimpered Mildred, 'but I just couldn't resist the temptation. It was the chance of a lifetime.'

'Hang on a minute,' said Dover and popped back into the dry again. 'We've got one that wants to talk,' he groaned to MacGregor. 'It's as cold as charity out there. That girl must be damned near freezing. Any chance of a cup of char?'

'I'll see to that,' burbled Mr Whitbread eagerly. 'You're a good man, I can see that.' He beamed at Dover. 'God grant that your endeavours be crowned with success, if not in this world then in the next.'

Dover turned to MacGregor before plunging out once more through the window. 'And get rid of *him!*' he ordered in an unnecessarily loud voice. Mr Whitbread forgave him with an indulgent smile.

'All right,' bawled Dover, and the rain-sodden shoes jumped again, 'let's be having it! And just remember I haven't got all day to spend listening to you rambling on.'

Mildred Denny had obviously been thinking her story over and tried to make it as coherent as possible. 'I'm private secretary to the director of the laboratory,' she began.

'I know that!' snapped Dover. 'Get on with it!'

'Well, these two reports landed on my desk at the same time, you see, for me to type out the letters to the doctors. Well, naturally I read them through. I'd got to type them out, hadn't I?' she added defensively. 'I picked up John's first— John Perking, that is. Well, naturally, I was interested. John's an old friend of mine. I knew him very well long before he married and naturally I still take an interest in him. Well, this report said that there was nothing the matter with him. You know— there was no medical reason why he shouldn't be able to be a father. Well,'— her voice took on a self-righteous note — 'I was very glad for him. I know how badly he and Cynthia wanted a child. Anyhow, before I typed out John's report I thought I'd get the routine confirmations of pregnancies out of the way first. And there, right on the top of the pile, was one for Mrs Cynthia Perking.' Mildred began to blubber. 'Well, it was just too much, it really was! She's always had everything, Cynthia has. It's always dropped straight into her lap. And now she was even going to have a baby! That'd mean the end of the estrangement with her father and she'd be back living in the lap of luxury just like she was before. Not that I really begrudged her that, but it just wasn't fair that she should get my money as well.'

MacGregor was tugging at Dover's coat tails. Dover willingly pulled his head in from outside.

'The padre's got the tea, sir.'

Mr Whitbread, smiling all over his face, stepped forward

with a large steaming mug of tea in his hands. Dover grabbed it. Mr Whitbread looked worried.

'How are you going to get it out to the poor girl?' he asked.

The fatuous question died on his lips as Dover raised the mug and tipped the contents noisily down his throat.

'Ta, very much,' said Dover, handing the mug back. 'I wouldn't mind the same again since you've asked. And you might see if you can get a drop of the hard stuff to lace the next cup with. It's as cold as Hades out there.'

The rain-sodden shoes were still clinging to the gutter.

'Carry on!' Dover shouted up at them. 'What's all this about Cynthia Perking getting your money?'

But Mildred Denny was weakening. 'I don't want to stay out here any longer,' she complained. 'I'm getting soaked to the skin.'

'You're not the only one,' snapped Dover. 'Well, come on down then! It'll suit me.'

The rain-sodden shoes shuffled about. The guttering creaked and sagged even further. Dover, squeamish, closed his eyes. There was a frantic scrabbling on the tiles of the roof.

'I can't get down!' Mildred Denny's lament came loud and clear. 'I'm stuck! I daren't move!'

'Women!' muttered Dover and relayed the news to Mac-Gregor. 'The stupid cat's come to her senses but now she's stuck and can't get down.'

'Oh, dear! Oh, dear!' Mr Whitbread was still hanging around. He went on bleating helplessly until Dover cut him short.

'Well, now's your chance, padre! Just let me clear out of the way and then you can nip out and do your rescue act.' Dover leered wickedly at the chaplain whose face suddenly matched his clerical collar for shining whiteness. 'I reckon they'll give you a medal for this. And, believe me, you'll have earned it! You wouldn't get me out on that roof for a million quid.'

'Oh, dear!' said Mr Whitbread in quite a different tone of voice. He clutched his chest as a last straw. 'Oh, dear, I do believe I'm going to have one of my attacks. Nothing to worry about, of course, but my heart isn't quite as strong as it used to be. If I could just sit down ... oh, thank you so much!'— this as MacGregor pulled up a packing case—'So kind! I'll just sit here quietly. Don't you bother about me. I'll be as fit as a fiddle again in two or three hours.'

Dover wrinkled his little black moustache contemptuously. 'Tell 'em to fetch the fire brigade, laddie!'

While the Pott Winckle fire brigade was wending its leisurely way towards the Pott Winckle hospital, Dover lent an ear to the remainder of Mildred Denny's confession. As he pointed out to her, she might as well spit out the rest while she was waiting.

The juxtaposition of the laboratory reports on Mildred's secretarial desk had proved too much for her. She'd had a lifetime of seeing Cynthia get everything and the knowledge that her cousin's good fortune was going to continue unabated produced a crisis. 'I don't know what came over me,' said Mildred from her chilly perch on the roof, 'but suddenly I saw it all quite clearly. After all, I've got to think of my future, haven't I? I don't want to finish up in one of these twilight homes with nothing but my old-age pension to live on. And you know what the hospital service is like—they don't pay you enough to keep body and soul together, never mind put anything aside for a rainy day.'

'I do wish you'd get to the point,' grumbled Dover. 'I'm getting a crick in my blooming back leaning out like this.'

'But money is the point!' retorted Mildred. 'I would never have dreamt of doing it if it hadn't been for the money.'

'What blasted money?' groaned Dover.

'*My* money, of course. Well, it will be mine when Uncle Quintin dies. And now'—she chuckled softly to herself—'and now it will be *all* mine, won't it? I shan't have to share it with Cynthia. Not now!' she added with great satisfaction. 'Of course, Uncle Quintin's the one to blame, really. He should never have made such a stupid will. Oh, I know what you're going to say: Cynthia's just as much Uncle Quintin's great-niece as I am. Or, she was. Well, in a way you're right. Both our mothers were Sinclairs, but my mother didn't marry

Daniel Wibbley, did she? If she had done and if I was heiress to all the Wibbley money, I wouldn't have expected to get half the Sinclair inheritance too, would I?'

'I wish you'd pull yourself together,' said Dover, growing more and more impatient. 'Do you mean that Cynthia Perking was going to inherit some money from your joint Uncle Quintin?'

'Yes, of course.'

'How much?'

'Well, nobody really knows. About ten thousand pounds, I think. But I'd have only got half of that, wouldn't I? Cynthia would have got the other half and five thousand pounds to her – why, it would have been chicken feed. But, the way Uncle Quintin's left it, if one of us dies the other gets the lot. Do you understand? Of course, one of us would have to die before Uncle Quintin does, otherwise it wouldn't work.'

'Clear as mud,' said Dover scathingly.

'Well, Uncle Quintin was a bit gaga when he made it,' admitted Mildred. 'Now he's completely potty of course and they've had to get a power of attorney or something for him. That's why there wasn't any other way, you see. If Uncle Quintin was sane I could have gone and talked to him and told him that Cynthia didn't need a measly five thousand pounds when she was going to get all her father's money, but that it would make all the difference in the world to me. I'd have got him to change his will and leave me the lot, I'm sure I would. Then', she added tearfully, 'I shouldn't have had to get rid of Cynthia, should I?'

Dover retreated from the window. 'Can you hear what she's saying out there?' he asked MacGregor.

MacGregor shook his head. 'Not a word, sir.'

Thank God for small mercies, thought Dover.

'By the way, sir,' said MacGregor quickly before Dover disappeared again. 'There are all sorts of people who keep coming to the door and demanding to know what's going on. We've had the hospital secretary, the matron, the chairman of the board of governors, the … '

'Yes,' said Dover, 'very interesting. Well, tell 'em everything's under control. And, while you're about it, tell that parson fellow I'm still waiting for my second cup of tea.'

Mildred Denny began once more to tell her story to the back of Dover's head. 'No, of course I didn't actually murder Cynthia with my own two hands! Don't be silly! Besides, I've got an alibi. I was working late in the office that night. I was hard at it till half past six and Dr Moreton and at least two of his assistants can vouch for me. So there!'

'Then why', asked Dover wearily, 'do you keep saying you did kill her?'

'Because', said Mildred with a woman's logic, 'I did. If it hadn't been for me John would never have hurt a hair of her head. Somebody had to sort of prompt him.'

'You?'

'Well, of course! I say, you're a bit slow on the uptake, aren't you? Are you sure you're a policeman? Now, where was I? Oh, yes – the day when both the lab reports arrived on my desk. Well, I suddenly had this flash of pure inspiration. I'd thought about getting rid of Cynthia before, of course. I didn't really like her, you know. But I could never work out a foolproof way of doing it. But, with those two lab reports, it was just too easy. All I had to do was alter John's. Where it said negative, I just had to put positive. Or was it the other way round? Anyhow, it doesn't matter. I just had to put the opposite. It was all so simple. I typed out a special carbon copy with the right information on to go in our files – just in case – and that was that. I knew perfectly well what would happen. John would be told he was sterile at the very moment Cynthia was told she was pregnant. I knew John. He'd go mad if he thought Cynthia had been unfaithful to him. And' – she sniggered disagreeably – 'he did, didn't he? And I knew he'd rather die than tell anybody why he'd done it. He was always rather sensitive about that kind of thing. I was ever so surprised when I saw he'd actually gone to consult a doctor about it. Oh, I knew his lips would be sealed – to the grave.'

Moodily Dover contemplated the rain water dripping off

his bowler. He sighed. Just his rotten luck, wasn't it? 'And you did all this for a lousy five thousand?' he asked.

'I shall get ten thousand now when Uncle Quintin dies. Do you realize how much that is? Invested in building societies it'd bring me in, at four and a quarter per cent, four hundred and twenty-five pounds a year, tax free. That's if I took the interest twice yearly, of course. If I let it accumulate and if the rate went up to, say four and a half or even five per cent, I should get something round ... '

The distant wail of the fire-engine siren interrupted her calculations.

'Are they coming to rescue me?' she asked.

'I suppose so,' Dover said glumly.

'What's going to happen? Will they send me to prison?'

'They ought to boil you in oil!' growled Dover. 'Why on earth didn't you keep your trap shut? You'd have been as safe as houses.'

'But I thought you'd found out what I'd done. When you phoned up to say you were coming to the laboratory I naturally assumed you'd discovered everything.'

'Yes,' agreed Dover, 'well, we had, more or less. There were just a few loose ends that needed tying up. We'd have got the whole picture soon enough.'

'Well, there you are then, aren't you? I thought the only thing left was for me to kill myself. I wish those firemen would hurry up. I'm getting frightened up here. And I'm cold and wet, too. How long will they send me to prison for?'

Dover was silent for a few moments. The fire engine came hurtling round the corner of the hospital building. It was now or never.

'Do you want some advice, miss?'

'Oh,' gasped Mildred, 'that's awfully kind of you! You've listened so sympathetically and patiently and everything. If you could give me some advice, I should be so grateful.'

'If I was you, miss,' said Dover slowly ...

'Yes?'

' ... I'd jump!'

MacGregor helped Dover away from the window. 'Well, sir?' he asked eagerly.

'The firemen'll get her down.'

'But what's she been saying, sir?'

'Oh, just nattering on about this and that. You know what women are, especially hysterical types like her.'

'But she must have said something, sir.' MacGregor looked at Dover with frustration and scepticism. 'I mean, she is Cynthia Perking's cousin, she was friendly with Perking himself before he got married and here she is, actually working in this laboratory where both those tests were processed—there must be a tie-up somewhere, surely, sir?'

'Got that list of trains back to London, laddie?'

'Well, yes, sir.'

'What time's the next?'

'Four fifteen, sir.'

'We'll just make it. Come on!'

'But, sir,'—Dover had already got the door open—'we've got to go and see Mr Wibbley.'

'Who says?' Dover was halfway down the corridor.

'Mr Wibbley himself, sir. He sent a message by the chauffeur. I didn't like to interrupt you when you were talking to the girl but he was most insistent. Mr Wibbley wants to see you in his office at the factory at the earliest possible moment.'

Dover pressed the button to summon the lift.

'And the Chief Constable, sir! He wants to have a word with you, too. He says he doesn't want to interfere but he would like to be kept in the picture. If you could spare him the odd half-hour this evening … '

The lift doors opened and Dover stepped out on to the ground floor. He addressed the receptionist who was still on duty at her desk. 'Any taxis knocking around, miss?'

'I can telephone for one if you wish. It will cost you four pennies.'

'Tell him to come round to the side door, there's a good girl. Well, don't just stand there, MacGregor! Give her the money.'

MacGregor caught up with Dover just in time to open the side door for him.

'I suppose that bloody chauffeur's hanging around at the front still,' said Dover. 'No point in letting him see us. I'll bet he's been reporting every blooming move we've made back to old Wibbley.' He laughed without humour. 'I wish I could see that so-and-so's face when he finds out. He'll have a fit.'

'Finds out what, sir?'

'That his precious son-in-law'll have 'em in tears when his case comes up for trial. There'll be so much flaming sympathy for him it wouldn't surprise me if the jury didn't bring him in not guilty.'

'But, I don't understand, sir.' MacGregor was thoroughly bewildered. Much to Dover's satisfaction.

'You will, laddie, you will!'

Before MacGregor had time to press his inquiries any further there was an imperious miaow. The large black hospital cat came speeding towards them, tail erect and demanding to have the door opened for him.

During his time at the hospital he had grown fat and sluggish. He'd grown accustomed to receiving only affection and kindness from the human beings with whom he came in contact. His reactions weren't as sharp as they should have been

'Bloody animal!' snarled Dover and swung a nifty foot.

The cat saw it coming and ran.

He didn't *quite* make it.